❧Votive Candles☙

<u>Fiction Series</u>
The Alex Evercrest Series
The River Front
The Girl on The Grill
Missing
Maggot
Racist
Votive Candles
Windy City
Country Road
Pool of Blood
Sins of the Daughter
Body Parts
The Skull Collector
The Vanishing
The Shadow Fighter
Moonshine
Grief's Trajectory
The Magic Touch
Northern Lights
Alex Evercrest Heroine
Alex Evercrest Collection Two
New Direction
A Family Affair
Disruption
The St. Lebuinnus Church Murder

A Brian O'Neil Novel
Hawaiian Phoenix
Moon Curser
Death Broker

The Problem Solver Series
Solutions
Drug Lords
Border Crosser
The Problem Solver Collection

<u>The Taelo Series</u>
Taelo: The Early Years
Taelo: The Golden Feather
Taelo: Journey of Discovery
Taelo: Dangerous Passage
Taelo: Condor Clan Slingers
Taelo: Circumvention
Taelo: The Journey of Sages
Taelo: Collection
Taelo: Future Leaders Journey

<u>A Taelo Story:</u>
White Swan and Quiet Pheasant
The Child's Name
Floating Cloud
Quiet Rabbit
Busy Bee
Little Otter & Talking Wren
Broken Spear
Burley Bear & Meadow Flower
Taelo Story Collection

<u>Science Fiction</u>

Ron Mueller

The Savitar Series:
Journey's End
Savitar
Confluence
Savitar Series Collection

Bram Nielson Series
The Fold
The Message
Fold Wormhole
Negative Fold
Ripples in Time
Bram Nielson Collection

<u>Single Science Fiction Books:</u>
Current Past and Future
The Event
The Door
Viajante 7

ഔ*Votive Candles* ൽ
By: *Ron Mueller*

Around the World Publishing LLC
Cincinnati, Ohio

Dedicated to those wronged by the Church.

<u>*Table of Contents*</u>

Ron Mueller

1 A Step Outside

Alex sipped on her drink and looked at Matt. He quizilled his eyebrows as he took in her gaze and took a sip of his drink. She smiled and explained that she was thinking about the last case and how significantly being a victim of a hate crime had affected her.

She said that it was the first time she had thought of herself as a victim.

She explained that it had caught her unprepared to be attacked for her color. She had come to expect and handle all forms of discrimination but had not anticipated someone trying to kill her for being Black.

She knew that her survival did not change the fact that a significant number of such people continued hold onto their hateful beliefs.

She was sure their own insecurities fueled their beliefs and attitudes.

She added that their enrollment at the university in the class on the History of the Black experience in the building of America was really refreshing her memory and it was broadening her understanding of what their race had endured.

She made the point that even as they endured they had made significant contributions to the growth of the country.

She realized that being one of only four students in an all-white school and being raised in an all-white affluent neighborhood made her experience closer to being white than being black.

Throughout her growing up she had periodically sensed and experienced social discrimination but in what she now realized was a much more subdued fashion than the majority of persons of color.

Her continuing higher education had also lifted her up to a social level where discrimination was practiced in a subtle manner.

The fact that no long term Cincinnati police member had been willing to be her partner in the detective unit was another time that discrimination was blatantly obvious.

Trey had been hired into the detective unit because he said he preferred to be second on the team and that person's color did not matter.

She had immediately known that he would be the person she could count on. He had been a Marine that had fought in Iran and had seen battle. He had been recognized for his bravery and had been awarded the purple heart. From their first meeting she felt that they would make a great team.

She had been repeatedly attacked by gunmen trying to kill her. She had been lucky, and her personal skill had made them all pay the ultimate price.

Every time she need backup, Trey was there

She told Matt that it had been a quiet period at work and that she knew that the Chief was guiding most of the work away from her.

He was in his protective mode.

She had welcomed this but was now ready to get back to the work she loved.

She shared that, Trey, her work partner, had commented that he had spent more time with family in the last few weeks and that she should get attacked more often.

She had replied that she loved him too.

The two of them had become a team that was looked upon as the top team in the detective unit.

Even Trevor, with whom she sparred verbally every time they were around each other had complimented her on the way she handled her cases.

She and Trey were both AA members and supported each other in staying on the dry side. She had been an AA member since her college days and over a year of working with Trey she had gotten him to join. It had made a difference for him, and he thanked her for her persistence in getting him to go with her.

They also spent time with activities that reduced the stress of their jobs.

Alex was "Aunt Alex" to Trey's son Nolan. She and his wife, Lindsey, were good friends. They often had lunch, and it seemed that two weekends a month, Alex and Matt were over to Trey's house for dinner.

Annie, the young woman she had rescued from her fifteen-year captivity in the Pennsylvania forest, now a very successful, wealthy artist and her two daughters, Linda and Lorie were often at these gatherings at Trey's.

Both of the girls also referred to her as, "Aunt Alex."

Annie had recently purchased a home on seven and a half acres in Indian Hill. The housewarming had been a grand event. Annie had thanked Alex for saving her and for getting her into painting professionally.

Alex brought her mind back to Matt and took in his green eyes and smiled. She was surrounded by the people she loved and who gave her inner power and inspiration.

She thought to herself, "What more could a person want?"

She had made a point of supporting one of the best restaurants in Cincinnati because it had been the scene of her first shooting.

This evening, she was sitting at the same table and facing in the same direction as the time she had been attacked.

Her weapon was in her purse.

She had put the purse straps on her chair and had sat on them so that the purse acted as a holster.

She suddenly realized that someone was walking toward her table. She quietly told Matt to do exactly as she told him.

She made certain that the individual was not brandishing a weapon. He was well dressed and had a smile on his face.

She still put her hand on her weapon.

He excused his interruption and introduced himself as John Williams. He explained that he had come to dinner with his companion. He pointed to a very good-looking lady sitting alone at a table and introduced her as Hanna Hillman. He went on to say that he had recognized the two of them because of the news casts in which they had both recently appeared.

He stopped and then declared that he need her help and would she consider doing some investigation to bring two criminals to justice.

Alex released the grip on the revolver in her purse. She had never been approached in quiet this manner. She was intrigued but she made the point that her assignments were given to her by her boss, and that John should contact the Cincinnati Chief of Detectives, Bruce Johnson.

John looked at her and knew that he had to provide enough information so that she would take on his case. He replied that he had already made an official request that would most likely be in the Chief's hand by Monday morning. He asked if he could sit for a moment and explain why he needed her to take the case.

Alex pointed to the chair to her right and said he had five minutes.

She watched as John's face took on a strained look. She immediately sensed that the case had a personal aspect to it.

She listened as he explained that the request was in two parts. One was to find and return a Priest that had failed to respond to a Grand Jury subpoena. The priest was being charged for being a pedophile. John explained that he had been an Altar boy in the church and had been one of the young boys that had been a victim of this priest. He had removed himself from the case and Hanna was now handling it. There were three persons that were potential witnesses.

This was the part of his request that he most wanted help with. It was to find and return this priest to face the Grand Jury and hopefully then be brought in front of a jury of his peers and be tried for his crime.

He said the second help request was due to a lawyer that she should be somewhat familiar with, a Samuel Ellington III.

This was a case that he was personally handling that consisted of a peculiar divorce situation. A wealthy individual and his wife were in the process of getting a divorce. It was a friendly split, and she was to receive half of their combined wealth. During the divorce she died but there were certain indications that there may have been foul play. John explained that he had reviewed the divorce agreement, and everything was fair and equitable. His client had put his deceased wife's portion into a Charity Remainder Trust that would allocate its money and give it to a charity that she had always supported.

The situation was that Samuel Ellington III had accused his client, the husband, of murder and of illegally retaining control of her wealth.

The help he was asking for was for Alex to use her investigative skill to find out who was behind the charge and who would benefit financially if the money that was in the Charity Remainder Trust was released to them.

Alex looked at John and smiled. She quietly informed John that she would consider taking the cases if they came officially to her.

She also let him know that she was just recovering from a hate crime and knew how hard it was to get over feeling like a victim.

John thanked her and asked if he could buy the two of them a drink.

Alex smiled, thanked him for the offer, and let him know that both their drinks were Pellegrino and she pointed to a large bottle that was still half full and declined the offer.

John said that it was a pleasure talking to her, thanked her and returned to his table.

Matt looked at her and asked if she thought the case would make it to the Chief's desk.

Alex looked across the room to where John was sitting down across from his companion. She replied that it would be a first, but she figured that John was the type of person that knew how to work the legal system. He had the same presence as her mother who was also a lawyer that was mostly on the winning side.

That Sunday, Alex for some unknown reason, decided to attend Mass.

It was the first time since she had moved to Cincinnati.

She went in early.

She lit a Votive candle and made a prayer for guidance.

She wanted guidance on whether to pursue the wayward priest.

The nightmare she had experienced about this situation was one where she was the victim.

She decided to light a second Votive candle and ask for guidance on her romance with Matt.

Her relationship was one that she cherished and wanted to keep growing.

She sat through a sermon and realized that hearing the same story over and over was why she had stopped going to Mass. She was sure she had heard every version of sermon and every twist that the priests tried to enlist in giving a fresh sermon.

They needed the help of some good writers.

<u>2 The Choice</u>

J ohnnie thought back on how his relationship with Alex had changed his life. He had returned from Vietnam and had been rejected by a society that he had fought for in a country that he had never heard of against a people that as a famous black boxer had said and went to jail for, "the people in Vietnam are not a threat to the United States."

He had worked hard at every job that he had been able to land but seemed to be the first to be laid off when business went south.

He did not realize that when he had witnessed the brutal killing of a young lady that his life had taken an upward turn.

He was sure he would be dead within a couple of weeks.

When the wrong person was arrested for the killing, he knew he had to come forward and correct the error.

He was rejected by an ass of a lawyer with the ridiculous name of Samuel Ellington III that was representing the man accused of murder. He wondered if he was the third ass in his family.

After being ignored, he had then remembered the young black rider that passed the Cincinnati Library on a bicycle early each morning. He knew she was a cop because he had followed her and watched her lock her bike into the bike rack at the entrance to the police station.

He had stopped her and told her his story.

She had believed him.

She had hired him as her part time computer analyst.

She had gotten him his apartment superintendent job in the apartment building that she lived in.

She had changed the downward trajectory of his life.

She had saved him.

The recent attack on her because she was black had enraged him and he had worked harder than he had ever done before to make sure that the attackers were brought to justice.

As he expected Alex closed that case and was now recovering. He knew that she was seeing an psychologist to deal with the fact that she had been a victim just because of her color.

He had decided that he would take a personal hand in trying to keep her safe. He had decided to use some of his Vietnam experience as the point person on a march and became the point bicycle rider on Alex's way to work.

This morning, he was outfitted in a purple and black riding outfit. He was her lead on her ride to work. He had spent a small fortune on his bike.

It was a different brand but of the same caliber that Alex rode.

He had declared that he was protecting his lifestyle and that she would have a riding partner for as long as he could pedal.

He had been surprised when Alex had thanked him and had purchased a bike stand for him as a gift.

Johnnie insisted that they would alternate making the choice of the route they would take to work.

He also insisted that he be the point person. He pointed out that it had been his role in Vietnam, and he had survived it. His only demand was that he got to have the donut of his choice once they got to the station and that he was assigned a desk near her and Trey.

Alex laughed and agreed to his demands. She made the point that she would probably not have survived in Vietnam and from what she knew the women from North Vietnam were fierce fighters that would have challenged her.

She welcomed Johnnies partnership. She was still struggling to overcome the feeling of being a victim of a hate crime. Her sessions with the department psychologist were continuing but she had pushed them to be done either at a lunch session or in morning coffee break session.

Her psychologist was slowly becoming a friend.

The sessions helped her, and it helped with her AA adherence. She had enlisted Trey for periodic participation in her meetings with her psychologist.

He had commented that it helped him as well.

This Monday morning after changing into her work clothes she sat down and was sipping her coffee.

Trey walked in with his cup and a half of a bear claw. He handed the other half to her.

Johnnie had a jelly filled donut well on the way to completion.

Bill and Trevor had their coffee and donuts.

The five of them were sharing their normal morning banter when the volume from the Chief office caused them to stop and look at each other.

Trevor asked if Alex's car was still in the lot and that it had not been blown up.

Bill commented that a new case that the Chief was not in agreement with had probably arrived on his desk.

Alex looked down at her coffee but remained silent. She wanted to call Matt and let him know that John's case had made it to the Chief.

She wondered how it had been delivered. Usually, the cases came from the coroner after a killing. This one was coming into the Chief in a form that seemed to anger him.

After what seemed like a moment of eternity the Chief opened his office door, pointed to Alex, and asked her to come in.

Alex listened to Bill as he said to remember that she had four people that would back up any decision she made. She quietly thanked him as she put her coffee down and turned to go into the Chief's office.

The Chief asked her to sit down so that he could explain a request that had come to his office. He had told his boss that he would leave the choice as to whether to take the case up to her. He said that line had caused his boss to get upset and threaten him.

Alex looked at the Chief and smiled and replied that of course she would take the case.

She had to keep his reputation intact.

He looked at her and asked how she could be sure she would take the case before she had even heard what it was.

She replied that she had gone to church for the first time since coming to Cincinnati and had received guidance that she was to take the case.

The Chief shook his head. He asked if she knew what the request was.

She replied that she would like to hear his take on it.

They both sat silently for a moment.

She was relieved when he opened a file that had a formal looking document that provided a written request. She wanted to understand the request in detail and how success would be measured.

The Chief looked at her and asked if he could call in the rest of her team so that he would only have to go through the details one time.

Alex nodded her head in agreement. She knew she would need the support of every one of the four sitting outside.

The Chief signaled for the rest to come in. He waited until everyone was seated. He commented that the assignment was different from their usual approach.

Trevor commented that it really must be since the office had been silent since Alex had been called in. He went on that usually everyone sitting outside hoped that the windows didn't blow out.

The Chief looked at him and nodded and replied that he had a mop and bucket assignment that would suit Trevor.

Then he opened the folder in front of him and slowly read the request.

Alex had turned her chair so that she could watch the four.

Bill gave small whistle as he listened to the details.

She saw Trevor's face go a little pale when the Chief went into the details that covered a Father Chris. She understood his reaction because she knew that he had been an Altar boy in his church and had asked his son if he would be interested.

The Chief pointed to Alex and shared that he was leaving the decision to her.

Alex nodded and said that it was a case that had come to her and had been explained by the person making the request. It had driven her to go to Church to ask for guidance. She shared that she had lit a Motive Candle and made a prayer.

It had been answered.

She asked if anyone had any questions.

Bill nodded and asked what he and Trevor should do.

Trevor commented that as always he had her back.

Johnnie smiled and replied that he already knew what her miracle request was going to be. He would get right on it once he walked his bicycle back to his apartment.

The Chief look at her and commented that he would cover the politics of the situation. He was a little upset at the route that the request had taken, and he wanted to know more about John Williams.

Alex looked at him and suggested that the politics would probably center on someone that had it in for John.

She suggested that the two of them work closely together to ensure that the top of the food chain was addressed versus the one asking for help.

She was sure that John had not divulged his own experience with Father Chris, and she said nothing about it.

She looked at Johnnie and said that she would need to find Father Chris's location.

She also wanted to know who was involved in the other part of the case that dealt with the money involved in the divorce case.

She added that Father Chris's location was the priority.

She looked at Bill and Travor and asked them to work with Johnnie and handle the money case.

She looked at Trey and said she needed his support on the religious side of the case.

She asked if anyone had an objection to calling the case, the Case of the Votive candles.

Travis commented that he was Baptist and wanted everyone to know he knew what Votive candles were and that he had never believed in them, but he was OK with giving the case that name.

Bill just shook his head and commented, "I put up with this guy every day."

Alex nodded and thanked the Chief for the gesture of letting her choose but like he often said, "things seem to come from above."

Not only did help come from above but Alex was soon to find out that it would also come from "The Angle on the Hill.

<u>*3 Exposure*</u>

As John stood to go back to his table, he thought back through the time that he had struggled to get over the experience that he had as an Altar Boy.

He had left the church.

He had tried going to college but was lost as to what he wanted to do.

He was mentally affected by his experience.

He decided to go into the military.

It was clear to him now that he was trying to prove to himself that he was still a man.

He thought about being a seal in the Navy.

Then about being a paratrooper in the Army.

He finally decided on being a Marine. The Marine Core seemed to espouse what he was looking for, Honor, Courage, and Commitment.

The leadership qualities of judgement, justice, integrity, unselfishness, knowledge, and loyalty, all reverberated with him.

The experience had helped him find his way. He had decided that he wanted to be a lawyer.

He had returned and went to college.

He once he graduated he had started his own practice and had slowly built it up to the point that he was generating the kind of income that he had in the past thought was beyond him.

He had not gone back to his church until he got the wedding invitation from one of his good friends.

The invitation triggered the action of describing Father Chris's wrongdoing and getting the charges to be placed in front of a Grand Jury.

The day of the wedding he went into the church and he had a special envelope that he was planning to deliver.

When he entered the Nave, he was immediately pulled back into his past.

Father Chris was to perform the wedding.

He was escorted to the in the second row on the bride's side. The stained glass window with the figure of Jesus with outstretched arms transfixed him and sent him back into his childhood.

He did not realized that he was being hit on by a gorgeous woman until after the wedding she stopped in front of him and directly asked if she could buy him a cup of coffee while they waited to go to the reception dinner.

He had been shocked and almost turned her down.

He had come with only two things in mind. One was to be at the wedding of the girl that he had first kissed but then she had only become his best friend.

And the second thing was to service Father Chris with the Grand Jury Subpoena.

He was glad that he had said yes to the third thing, the offer to go to coffee.

He was now into what he hoped would be a serious relationship with Hanna, the person that he was now walking back across the dining room to.

He took a long sip of his Moscato.

He let the sweet taste suffuse his pallet.

He had never shared his experience with Father Chris before. Somehow looking into Alex's almost black eyes had drawn out his story to a degree that surprised him. She had not probed or asked questions. She had listened. Listened in a manner that seem be a magnet for his mind.

Her greeting smile had been replaced with a look of concern. She had put her hand on his and held it there for the entire time he shared the request for her help.

She had not rejected his request but made the point that she did not select the cases she worked on.

Her boss did the selection.

He shared that he had put in a formal request that should reach her boss's desk over the weekend. He didn't say that he had pulled every string that he could to make the request a formal one.

He had done everything he could think of to get her to be put on the case.

He learned that the detective unit did not normally respond to requests like his.

He was told that they were not a detective agency.

He hoped that if they accepted his request the person sitting before him would be a superior sleuth to the detective agencies that had failed him.

Hanna looked at John and knew that he had experienced something significant. She looked over at the table where the person, Alex Evercrest, sat looking back over at her.

Alex nodded, took a sip from her glass, and then turned her attention to the man sitting across from her.

Hanna wondered about the long conversation that John had at that table. She hesitated and chose not to pursue the thought. She instead took a sip of her wine and put her hand on top of John's. He set his glass down and put his other hand on top of hers.

John took in Hanna's beauty and knew that soon he had to share the story that he had just related to a stranger, but he was not ready at the moment.

He chose to wait until he got confirmation that his request for help was accepted by the person he hoped would solve both requests.

It seemed that he paced the weekend away. Every time he set out to do something he replayed his early experience and then the telling of that experience to the black detective.

He wondered what about her had made him share something he had never shared with anyone.

Monday proved to be even more stressful. He was in the office but could not concentrate on the case that he was leading. His mind kept drifting back to sitting at the table and being probed by those black eyes.

Hanna came to his office to share that neither investigative agency had made any headway in locating Father Chris. She wanted to know what she should do next.

He suggested that she go before the Grand Jury and present her case. She had two willing witnesses that would provide the basis for a charge of Homophobic behavior.

He said nothing about his request to have Alex Evercrest take on both Hanna's and his case.

Hanna left the office concerned that she might get turned down by the Grand Jury.

She was hoping for more.

She knew that having Father Chris appear in court would make a significant difference.

She called her two witnesses and set up preparatory meetings. She wanted them to explain Father Chris's behavior concisely but clearly.

She had interviewed the parents of the current Altar boys, but they had denied any wrongdoing by Father Chris. All of them denied any bad behavior by Father Chris.

He had either stopped his behavior or the boys he was abusing had not shared their situation with their parents.

When John heard the voice on the phone his heart took an extra beat. He was hopeful that his request had been accepted but he also feared rejection.

He sat down and leaned his elbows on his desk.

He heard her voice ask whether he would have lunch with her and her partner at the same table where he had shared his story.

He closed his eyes as relief swept through his entire body.

He recovered his composure quickly and agreed if he could pay for lunch.

John had enough foresight to request that the person handling Father Chris's case be present.

He went to Hanna's office where he told her the story that he had shared with the Alex Evercrest the evening before.

He felt a sense of relief as he let the story unfold.

Hanna expressed her condolence and then asked if he were willing to be a witness in her case.

John responded that if it would make a significant difference to the case's outcome he would step up and be a witness but he pointed out that it was his office that was bringing the case in front of the grand jury, and it might work against them.

John then asked Hanna to have lunch with Alex Evercrest and her work partner.

Hanna smiled and shared that she knew the person that he was speaking of as "Cincinnati's Black Annie Oakley" and yes she looked forward to meeting her in person.

She made the point that she hoped that sleuthing was as strong a point for the detective as she was at being a dead shot.

John and Hanna walked in silence to the restaurant where they were to meet. It opened at eleven for a brief lunch period that was always well attended.

He was surprised when the Maître d' greeted him and said that Alex was waiting for him and then led him to the table. The person sitting across from her was a tall rather handsome person at least a foot taller than the person across from him.

He introduced himself and learned that Alex's partner's name was Trey.

He introduced Hanna as the person handling Father Chris's case.

This time the questions from Alex seemed endless. She shared that she had gone to Mass and had lit a Votive candle and asked for guidance on how to pursue Father Chris's case.

She smiled and added that the message she got back was that she should figure that out for herself. The one above was not into doing detective work, he was all knowing, and it was up to her to do her own sleuthing.

Hanna smiled and said that she now had a better understanding about the success that Alex had in pursuing the bad guys and closing cases.

She pointed out that her survival in the latest series of gun battles Alex was getting a lot of help from above.

Alex replied that her aim whether using a gun or tracking the bad guy was always focused on the target. She went on to explain that she did not work alone but leveraged the best support team that a person could possibly have.

She pointed at Trey and commented that he always had her back.

She shared that her analyst was an old Vietnam vet that always delivered his investigative miracles that led to her cases being solved.

He was her data analyst miracle worker.

She had some support team members that often competed with her, but they had agreed to work the money case that John was leading, and she and Trey would work the religious side.

Alex smiled and said that her boss claimed that many of her cases were sent from above.

She then said that the information probing was done, and they should concentrate on enjoying lunch.

She made the point that Hanna and John would each face additional questions by the two teams that would probe and learn the details that would close both cases successfully.

Hanna looked at John and commented that she felt much better about the upcoming Grand Jury session, and she would make sure to get them scheduled based on the timing Alex would determine.

25

3 Exposure

<ins>*4 The Fallen*</ins>

*T*he sight of John sent him more than twenty years back. He had not seen John for that long.

It brought back the memories of how much he had loved John and hand missed his absence.

John had been special.

Every time he looked at John his heart raced. He wondered what John had been doing all of the years that had gone by and why he had not come back to the church.

He hoped that after this he would get to see him more often and perhaps they could become friends.

He noted that even as an adult, John made his heart race.

The sermon and the wedding ceremony went well.

The bride was now a woman, but he remembered her Christening day.

He was pleased to be able to preside over her wedding.

It closed he loop for him.

After the wedding was over he led the procession out to the steps of the church.

He felt the warmth of the sun and knew that all was well.

He was shaking hands and wishing everyone a blessed day and then he was shocked when John served him the summons to be present in front of the Grand Jury to face charges of being a pedophile.

He was especially upset at having it done on the steps of the church.

That seemed so sacrilegious and improper.

He was relieved that John had not publicly said what the envelope that was handed to him was about, but he only said that he had been served.

After reading the letter in the envelope, he had not been able to concentrate on the afternoon sermon. He had stumbled multiple times during the sermon on the topic of personal responsibility.

All he could think about was that he needed to be somewhere else.

Once back in his office, he looked at the summons and knew that it was time for him to leave the city and to disappear.

He decided that he would seek to work with his friends in the south.

He would go on sabbatical and never return to the US. He submitted his papers to the diocese to go on a sabbatical so he could renew his faith.

He would do that and not have to face the embarrassment of being exposed.

He carefully laid out his trip. He wanted to make sure that he could not be found.

He planned to go to Mexico where a longtime friend had a church.

He had three other friends spread out through South America that had their own churches.

He planned to stay a few years at each location.

He would spend the rest of his days going from church to church.

It was a good end to serving the church and its faithful.

He sent a text to his first friend and inquired if he could come for a few months as he refreshed his faith.

The yes answer triggered him to schedule his departure.

He booked a round trip out to the Teton Area. He did not plan to ever use the return portion of his ticket. He would spend a few days touring Yellow Stone National park then he would go south to the Grand Canyon and stay there for several days. He wanted to get out of the US but did not want to attract any attention and he did not want to appear in a hurry.

He made reservations using a different name at each place. He always paid cash. There would be no credit card trail.

He hoped in this way to make it impossible to be tracked.

He made his journey in civilian clothes and felt that he had successfully blended in as a single tourist. He felt that he blended in well with the general population.

The life of a priest was one of being frugal. All his belongings fit into a large suitcase and a carryon. He knew that he would find anything else that he needed when he got to where he was going.

His stay at Yellow Stone put him in touch with nature.

It seemed that he was closer to his maker.

He prayed,. Thanked him, and asked for forgiveness.

He went on several hikes and took in the glory that God had forged on Earth.

He felt that he was a good priest and had provided guidance for many souls.

He then took the bus to the Grand Canyon and spent a few days there. He rode a donkey down into the canyon and tried not to think about falling. He decided that he had not really enjoyed that trek.

From the Grand Canyon area, he took a bus to the US, Mexico border at El Paso.

He had withdrawn his entire savings from his bank in Cincinnati and was carrying more cash than he wanted.

He stayed in El Paso long enough to put the cash he was carrying into several of the banks there. He had to use more than one bank so that he could put in an amount that would not trigger any flags or be noticed. He stayed for several days and returned to the three banks he had selected and deposited the money in less than five-thousand-dollar sums. He always use a different teller to deposit the money.

He would later open an account at each location that he stayed and have some of the money transferred from the El Paso banks to his new account.

Finally, he was ready to cross the border. He waited until there was a large group of people crossing back into Mexico and fell in behind them.

His crossing was a non-event.

Once across he took a bus to his final destination. He was sure that no one would be able to trace him and find the church he was going to.

He felt a surge of relief to be out of the US.

He felt relieved to be moving on. He knew the church hierarchy would not divulge his whereabouts. Where abouts that he had not specifically identified. So, they would be absolutely clueless.

He figured he would never face the Grand Jury in Cincinnati.

He relived his experience with John's rude and ill-timed manner of serving the summons.

He wished he could tell John how contemptible and unprofessional that had been.

It also seemed to reflect a weakness in John that he wondered about.

It was a relief to him that he was moving on. He would concentrated his energy on doing good work as he began a new part of his life's journey.

He felt that he was a good priest and had provided excellent guidance for many souls.

He knew that he harbored one fatal weakness, and he prayed daily for forgiveness.

He had never been unkind to any of the boys that he had groomed.

He had been generous and had given them many gifts.

He kept going over his transgressions and seeking guidance. He prayed that at the end of his days he would be forgiven and not have to face the black angels of death.

He kept repeating to himself that his savior was one that practiced forgiveness.

He noted that it was a month since he had left Cincinnati. He was becoming more confident in his ability to disappear. There was nothing to indicate that anyone was trying to catch him.

The crossing into Mexico and his subsequent bus ride to Monterrey were uneventful.

Monterrey was larger than he had anticipated. It was closer to a Cincinnati sized town than what he had imagined.

He located a place to live that was within walking distance from the church. He had enough cash to pay for six months rent.

He found a bank near the church and opened an account and had a portion of his savings transferred in from El Paso.

His friend offered a position that would pay him a stipend that would cover his living expenses.

The irony of the fact that he was asked to teach and council the group of children that was under the care of the church did not escape him.

He was sure that it was a test from above.

About a dozen of the children ranging from five to fifteen were housed by the church in an apartment like facility.

During the day, another dozen came to be watched.

He was relieved that none of the kids attracted him.

He concentrated on teaching them and on making sure they were healthy. His meetings, with the parents of his day children, were friendly and he felt that he had made a good transition to a new life.

Father Jones, as he was now going by, prayed for guidance and strength as he carried out his new role.

Life took on a rhythmic routine. A periodic movie, daily lessons in Spanish, an early morning and an evening walk and the daily tutoring of the kids.

At his six month celebration he went to one of the best restaurants in the city and enjoyed a light dinner and drank a bottle of the best Sauvignon wine. It was the first time he had splurged on himself since having left the States.

He felt good at having made the transition and planned never to look back.

He would now live a life of helping the people in Latin America.

If Father Jones had known who had decided to return him to Cincinnati, he would not have celebrated with much gusto. The future was much darker than he thought it would ever be and the hand from above was guiding his pursuer.

His sunny day was about to be transformed into lightening, thunder, hail, and rain.

And in the near future the taste of his wine would be like the taste of vinegar.

5 *On the Trail*

*A*lex had asked Johnnie to track down the missing Father Chris. She had gone to the leaders of the church and was told that Father Chris had taken a sabbatical to renew his faith and that where he had gone was not on record and in any case could not be divulged.

She asked Johnnie to go on the search for the missing priest with every weapon he had at his disposal.

He thought about how to start and decided to start on the day John had given the subpoena to Father Chris on the steps to the church. It had been more than a month. He figured that was plenty of time to allow Father Cris to get out of the country. His guess was that it would either be Canada, or it would be Mexico.

He had access to every major data base and yet on his first search he came up empty. He had tracked down almost every Jones that had left Cincinnati by air, bus or train but had not found the one that was a priest.

He was certain that Father Chris was trying to cover his tracks. He felt like a tracker that had to follow game immediately after a major snowstorm.

The tracks were covered in snow and in his case the tracks were lost in time.

Every system he went into seem to archive their information differently and in differing formats. He plowed through them until there were only a handful of Jones that he need following up on.

In conversation with Alex, he listened as she made the point that Father Chris would not plan to return to Cincinnati and suggested looking at any Jones that had purchased a one way ticket to anywhere, in any fashion.

She made the point that he would not head directly out of the country, and she bet he would head west to some sort of resort or vacation spot.

He would most likely be trying to act like a tourist or vacationer and he would most likely be traveling light.

She suggested that he also look at any local bank that might have held his money.

He started with the bank account. He had learned that following the money seemed to almost always yield a good outcome.

He quickly found the account he was interested in and found that Father Chris had withdrawn close to two million dollars.

When he shared this with Alex she said she was surprised at the amount and wondered how a priest could have so much put away. She called the diocese and asked how much a normal priest was able to save.

She was at first told that information could not be shared.

Alex said that it seemed that she was being stone walled and that she was not asking about any specific priest and what she wanted to know was a general question. She left her name and number and asked the person on line to ask the church leadership for the information.

An hour later her phone rang, and she was given the information that on average, in the United States most priests made between twenty-five and thirty five thousand dollars. A few at the top end of the church hierarchy might hit one hundred thousand dollars.

Alex shared this with her team and conjectured that Father Chris was not only a Pedophile but most likely was also a thief that had skimmed money from the donation plates for a long time.

Johnnie was now looking at into three such Jones: one had taken a one way flight to Chicago, one out to Salt Lake City and one to Seattle.

He was able to learn the company that the person flying to Chicago worked for and that took him off the list

The one flying to Seattle turned out to be a woman.

That left the Salt Lake City flyer as the most likely one.

In Salt Lake city he searched every mode of transportation for a ticket paid in cash.

There was one bus ticket to from Salt Lake City to Jackson Wyoming purchased in cash. The clerk said that they could not share anything more than that.

Johnnie thanked him and searched Jackson for a hotel cash transaction.

He then queried hotel reservations paid in cash in Jackson. He found none in Jackson. He tried the park itself and got a hit. There was one reservation for three days.

This led Johnnie to check on cash paid bus tickets leaving Jackson.

He found one to the Grand Canyon.

Johnnie knew he was now on a roll and the footprints in the snow were getting easier to find.

He checked the hotels around the Grand Canyon and found that the one on the park grounds had one customer that had paid cash for a two day stay.

He then found the bus ticket to El Paso again paid in cash two days later.

He did a little jig and ate one of Alex's oatmeal cookies with a glass of milk as a payment to himself.

He let Alex know that Father Chris was in Mexico.

Johnnie felt fairly certain he had tracked down Father Chris, but he followed through on the other two possibilities.

He was able through their purchases with credit cards to quickly eliminate them.

Knowing the amount of money withdrawn from the Cincinnati bank, he spent some time searching for banks that had new accounts that had money put in during the time following the arrival of the bus from the Grand Canyon.

This took a much higher level of hacking, but he was able to find three banks that had a new account that had slowly been incremented with money deposits just slightly less than five thousand dollars at a time.

Johnnie totaled all the deposits and found that it added up to just a little less than two million dollars.

He noticed that one bank had transferred one hundred thousand dollars to a bank in Monterrey.

Johnnie smiled and knew that Alex would give him a tray of her cookies for what he had just learned.

He then focused on Mexican local news of a new priest arriving to a parish.

The quest seemed endless, but he continued the pursuit.

He shared his frustration with Alex.

Her response surprised him. She said that she had an "Angel on the Hill" in Mexico that might provide some help.

When they went online and Alex introduced Adrianna as the Angel on the Hill, Johnnie immediately understood. Alex had warned him not to divulge the reason that they were searching for Father Chris.

Alex's request was for Adrianna and her organization to see if they could locate the church where a Gringo priest had recently arrived and was active.

Adrianna introduced her brother, Adolfo and suggested he help in finding the Gringo Priest.

Adolfo said he would be pleased to work with Johnnie and said they should talk separately.

Johnnie hung up and a moment later Adolfo called and asked some details about the Gringo Priest. He then said he would call as soon as he had located him.

It was a little more than a day later that Johnnie received the message that such a person had recently arrived in Monterrey and that they were working in the capacity of teaching a class of students ranging from five to fifteen years old.

He was going by the name Father Jones

Johnnie was impressed with the speed at which Father Chris had been located.

He shared what he had learned and that he had continued to dig for additional information on the priest now being called Father Jones.

He was able to let Alex know the church, the apartment address and the bank account associated with him.

Johnnie confessed to having drained each of the accounts of the banks is El Paso and had it transferred to Alex's bank in her name and the name of the head of the diocese.

She had primary control of the account and was the only one that could with draw money.

Alex reacted with surprise as she listened to what Johnnie had uncovered. She thanked him for having been so thorough. She asked how he was able to close the bank accounts in El Paso.

Johnnie said that he hadn't closed the accounts but had only left one hundred dollars in each bank.

She asked him to contact the diocese and get the money transferred into their control and they could deal with how Father Chris had been able to accumulate that amount of money.

She was alarmed by the fact that Father Chris was teaching a class of young kids.

She commented that it bothered her that Father Chris was teaching a class of young kids.

She added that it bothered her more than the fact that he was a thief.

Johnnie was pleased with the fact that she gave him a hug and thanked him for providing her with all the information and that he really did deliver miracles.

She left his apartment and soon returned with a whole tray of a variety of cookies that she had baked.

He jokingly complained that he preferred large cash bonusses but held on to the tray as Alex tried to take it back.

He had to laugh when she asked him to help Bill and Trevor with another miracle for the money case and as the condition of his keeping the whole tray of cookies.

She said that now that she had all the information about Father Chris, she and Trey would deal with the religious case.

Johnnie contacted Bill and Trevor to see what they had learned and to get alignment as to how to proceed with them.

He was sure that Alex would quickly deal with the situation in Mexico.

His only worry was that she might go alone as she had done on a previous case when Trey, who had been brutally beaten, was in a coma. She had hunted down everyone who had been involved in brutally beating Trey and had dealt fairly but had taken the required action with each and in each case the person chose wrong.

He cornered the Chief and asked if Alex and Trey were both going to Mexico. He made the point that a team was safer than just one person going on their own.

He was relieved when the Chief assured him that this was an official case, and he would arrange for Alex and Trey to be there in an official capacity with supporting Mexican law enforcement.

Johnnie left the Chief's office and went over to Bill and Trevor and let them know that he had located Father Chris and that Alex and Trey would soon be going to bring him back.

Trevor commented that he hoped for Father Chris's sake that when given the choice he would choose to obey Alex versus trying to shoot her.

Trevor would later not believe what Father Chri had tried and that he had lived to come back for trial.

6 Treed

The week was wearing down Alex's patience. Johnnie was working hard at trying to find to where in the world Father Chris had run. She concentrated on staying out of his hair. She was pleased that he gave her frequent progress reports.

She made every type of cookie that she knew how to bake and took them down to his apartment as a way to interrupt and to learn of his progress. She enjoyed sharing a cup of coffee and listening to his chatter on how he had found the trail of Father Chris's nearly invisible travel route.

Johnnie made the point that Father Chris was using cash in his attempt to stay under the radar. He said that Father Chris was just not aware that technology had advanced to where time stamps associated with each of the locations and that cash purchases were discernable if matched with time.

He pointed out that cash was so seldom used that they stood out more than credit card transactions.

It was a challenging process and nearly invisible. He called them Angel steps in the snow because he figured that to some higher power they might stand out, but they were not easily followed unless you were looking in the right database.

He smiled and commented that his superior intellect fueled by cookies was giving him the ability to see the steps.

Alex agreed with him and told him to stay on the trail and if he needed more cookies she would keep baking them.

The next morning Johnnie said that he needed help. He had traced Father Chris to the Mexican border and he knew he was in Monterrey because of the money trail.

He did not know where in Monterrey he might be.

Alex smiled and told Johnnie that she had an Angel in Mexico that might be able to help.

She contacted Adrianna and introduced her as the Angel on the hill. She made the point to him that there was no snow, but Alex was certain that the Angel would locate Father Chris.

Johnnie got it immediately because Alex had shared her story about her last trip to Mexico when she was hunting down the leader of the drug cartel.

After a brief introduction, he said that he was looking for help in finding a Father Chris that had recently arrived in Mexico.

Adrianna in turn introduced her brother, Adolfo, as the person that would be able to find any priest that didn't speak fluid Spanish.

Johnnie had thanked Adrianna and set up some separate time with Adolfo.

Adolfo called Johnnie and the two began working together. Adolfo wanted to know why Alex was after this priest but accepted Johnnie's explanation that all he could share was that Father Chris was to appear in front of a Grand Jury.

Johnnie said that Alex would fill in the details for he and Adriana in person when she traveled to Mexico.

Alex meanwhile informed Adriana that she would be coming to Mexico to escort Father Chris back to Cincinnati where he would be brought in front of a Grand Jury and that she would fill in the details when they met person to person.

Adriana replied that she understood that the walls had ears and they had both been in the room that had no ears.

Alex hung up and went to the Chief's office to work out the details of how the official and legal trip into Mexico would be handled. She wondered how different this trip would be compared to her last one.

Trey was present but remained silent during the meeting. He remembered worrying about Alex's last trip to Mexico when she had put her badge and gun on the Chief's desk and said that she was taking a sabbatical for a brief time.

Her sabbatical had not been about renewing her faith. It had been about avenging the fact that he was near death because of the person at the head of the cartel had been involved in putting him in the hospital.

Alex listened as the Chief suggested that Harold Zimmerman the DEA person in Chicago that Alex had befriended would be the person that could best make the arrangements. Harold was the same person that had helped Alex on her clandestine trip to Mexico.

When he learned who was online with him, Harold joked that he did not have enough bullet hole patches for his boat otherwise he would invite all of them to go fishing on the lake.

This was a reference to Alex's last visit home only a few months before where she and the yacht they were fishing from came under attack.

The yacht had suffered at least a dozen holes through the hull.

Trey spoke up and volunteered to supply the patches and that he was now also carrying body putty to cover the bullet holes in the car assigned to Alex.

Alex said that she accepted the fact that she seemed to be a target.

She then explained the current situation to Harold.

He in turn asked a few questions and then agreed to handle the border crossing both into Mexico and later back into the US. He said he would need an official request from the Cincinnati Police department to make it all happen. He suggested the crossing be at El Paso.

He said that he would need photos of both Alex's and Trey's passports as well as the official order for them to bring Father Chris back into the US.

The same afternoon Johnnie arrived in the office with a smile on his face.

Alex knew immediately that he had located Father Chris.

She listened as Johnnie explained that Father Chris was now using Father Jones as his moniker. The good news was that Johnnie had the specifics of every facet of Father Jones' current situation. The bad news was that he was teaching a class of young kids ranging from five to fifteen years old.

Alex reacted to the last bit of information by looking at the Chief and telling him she was leaving as soon as he and Harold could arrange the border crossing.

The Chief pointed out that it was Friday. He would have the required paperwork and documentation to Harold, but she should plan on leaving late in the morning on Monday.

He would make sure that everything would be expedited.

Alex knew that the wheels would not go much faster. She nodded and agreed that she would set up the trip and let him know the exact flight times.

She looked at Trey and asked if that worked for him.

Trey looked at her and replied that the timing worked for him. He said that he badly wanted to reign in the wayward priest and see him behind bars.

Alex agreed with him.

She had been surprised when John had confessed that he was one of Father Chris's victims. It meant that Father Chris had been active for more than twenty years.

She was soon to learn that Father Chris had probably been stealing from the donation pool for all that time as well.

She would also be surprised at the action that Johnnie had taken about the money.

Alex had taken on the case because of John's personal confession to being a victim otherwise she would most likely have passed it up.

She had experienced being a victim on her last case and was surprised how hard it was for her to share her feelings with Matt.

How John had brought himself to tell her of his personal experience amazed her.

She was not sure what to make of that situation.

7 Picnic

Thinking about children caused Alex to think about having a picnic. After sharing the idea with Matt and getting his agreement that it was a great idea the picnic seemed to flourish and blossom like a sunflower in the sun.

She envisioned an awning over a several picnic tables with a view of the river. The awning would provide shade if the sun was hot and if it rained they would be covered.

She called and invited Trey to a family picnic at the Riverfront and got immediate acceptance. She also called Annie, invited her, and got the same rapid acceptance.

She and Matt spent Saturday organizing the picnic and the menu. They decided on one large pizza, chicken wings and a cheese smothered backed potato, an apple pie with ice cream. They arranged for it all to be catered and set up in the park.

Matt asked if this was a special occasion. Alex gave a small laugh and replied that yes it was to be a family type picnic where the only sound she would hear would be the sound of children playing and having fun.

Matt said he understood.

He commented that after being around her that the sound of gunfire was too often present.

He had also been on EMT runs where she was the one, they were either rescuing or who in almost every case, she had done some unbelievable shooting.

Alex gave him a hug and said she was going to make a sign for the event.

She made a sign that had the words, "The Linda, Lorrie and Nolan Picnic." She knew Nolan would want to know why his name was last. She thought about this for a few moments and knew she had a good answer.

She made sure everyone knew where in the park that the picnic would be located.

She then thought about the guest list and decided to expand the occasion. She invited the Chief, Bill, Trevor, Abbie, and Johnnie. She added that all were welcome to bring their significant others. She added that they deserved a cheerful day as much as she did.

Matt said, "wow" and asked if she could afford the occasion. She said that she had a rainy day fund exactly for that.

She and Matt adjusted the entire menu to fit the new list. They were not worried about too much food figuring on sending it home with everyone that came. They also let the caterers know of the increase in the number of guests and made sure the awning cover was increased accordingly.

Saturday morning, as she and Matt were walking the park and locating where the awning, now much larger than the original, would be set up, when Alex decided to extend one more invitation. She invited John and Hanna whose cases she and the detective team were now actively working.

Alex returned to her apartment and decided on a long run in the gym.

Johnnie strolled in and sat down on the bench for the weightlifting machine. He had a cup of coffee in hand and said that it was the biggest weight he intended to lift but that he would watch her run and absorb the benefit of just thinking about being able to do what she did.

He asked about the picnic and asked if he could help in getting things ready.

Alex replied that neither of them needed to do anything but to enjoy the event. She explained that she had arranged the entire event to be catered.

Johnny let out a small whistle and asked if he could have a raise to match her salary.

Alex replied that she made less than he and that she was able to pull it off because of an Angel on the Hill.

She didn't explain about the mysterious large sums of money that were regularly deposited in her bank account. Most of it was redirected to a Charity Remainder Trust that each year provided most of its interest to various charities.

She had been surprised when John had brought up the fact that his client had moved money into such a trust.

She had set it up at the recommendation of the money manager she had engaged. He pointed out that it was a way to generate a yearly sum of money for the rest of her life and at the end the trust would be larger than when it began.

Johnnie smiled and replied that he understood the generosity of Angels and that his Angel rode her bicycle into work every morning.

Alex laughed and almost lost her footing on the treadmill. She told him to go back to his apartment and let her finish her run, in peace.

She and Matt decided that Saturday night dinner should be light and settled on a salad and wine in her apartment. They agreed that the picnic would most likely wreck any control they had on how much they ate.

Alex enjoyed a quiet evening sitting next to Matt as they both read and chatted. She relished the fact that neither of them was into the many shows that were a series of continuing stories that seemed to have no end.

The picnic began slowly, but as the kids got into playing some of the lawn games and the parents enjoyed the swings that gave them a wonderful view of the Ohio River it seemed to take on a life of its own. Everyone commented about it being the perfect venue. It was a pleasantly cool, sunny day and the breeze from the river kept everything enjoyable.

The only problem that arose was that someone had recognized Alex and soon the news media began to arrive.

Alex saw the Chief put in a call and soon three policemen arrived and held the media back.

Alex thanked him and then walked out to where the media was standing back. She explained that she had sponsored a family picnic. There was not much more that she could say about the gathering. She said that she would be glad to answer questions for fifteen minutes if afterwards they would disperse.

She was pleased that the group seemed willing. She fielded questions about her guests. The first question was about the sign hanging from the awning. They all wanted to know who Linda, Laurie and Nolan were.

It turned out that she got a rise from all the media when she explained that the picnic was for the three kids on the sign and that she was "Aunt" to all of them.

There were a few other personal questions then she thanked them for their attention and let them know that she was going back to the picnic.

Alex watched the cameras being put away and the news trucks slowly depart. Their presence had drawn a few spectators that now continued their walk or doing whatever they had been about.

Alex turned her attention back to the picnic. Nolan asked about why she had been talking to the news media. She shared that they were interested about the names on the sign. Nolan asked if anyone wondered why his name was last.

Alex replied that his name was last because not only was he a gentleman, but the best always come last.

Afterwards Lindsey came up to her and quietly complimented her on how she had fielded Nolan's question.

She then pointed out that Alex had become very proficient in handling the news media.

Alex commented that she had been surprised that the media had willingly departed.

The picnic was a slow enjoyable time, and it was late afternoon when the apple pie and ice cream was served.

Soon afterwards Alex supervised the packaging of all the extra food.

Lindsey and Annie ended up with the most.

Trevor lay claim to a six pack.

The Chief commented that it had been the first outing with her that he did not have to brandish a gun and that he looked forward to more such events.

He promised the next event would be at his place.

8 Border Crossing

lex had decided when she and Matt or she and Trey traveled anywhere it would be first class. Regular seats were OK for her but both Matt and Trey were tall and had long legs.

She had noticed Matt having to deal with someone in front of him reclining their seat.

On the next flight she had started the practice of flying first class.

The price always surprised her, but she figured she would rather be comfortable and arrive at the destination in decent shape. She also enjoyed the amenities that were provided in First class.

She knew it was splurging and she would not have been able to do it but the money that she was certain had been sent to her from her southern Angel that she had put into trust yield a larger income than she was making as a detective.

Alex had upgraded both Trey's and her ticket. Trey made a comment about being in the wrong que when she led the way to the First-class counter. She was cordially greeted and was asked who was taking the window seat and who would take the aisle.

She took the window seat and smiled as Trey put up his hand and said, "aisle."

They were surprised when they got to security that they were taken through a separate line. They were asked to check their weapons. They were informed that their weapons would be placed on board and returned to them on arrival in El Paso after they cleared security there.

Once the plane reached cruising altitude Alex reclined her seat and closed her eyes.

She thought about the last time she had gone to Mexico. It had been a clandestine trip. She had officially taken vacation but had worked with Harold Zimmerman to obtain the weapon she needed in Mexico.

Her mission was to arrest the head of the Gulf cartel! She thought now how crazy she had been and how lucky she was to be returning back to where it all had happened.

She never brought him in because he drew a gun and tried to shoot her in the back.

She had shot him between the eyes.

Ironically, his wife had saved her and had sent her to her brother who loaned her a car that she drove to the border.

Alex had been surprised when the wife had thanked her for delivering her to a new life. She was known to her brother by the code words "the Angel on the hill." This had been how he knew that his sister was the person communicating with him.

Adrianna had funneled many millions of the cartel's monies to a private account. With these funds, she established an organization focused on helping the millions of Mexican poor.

She also generously shared her money with her black Angel from the north.

This would be the first time that Alex would enter the compound that was now Adrianna's headquarter via the front gate and during daylight hours. The last time had been in the dark of night through a secret tunnel and up through the floor in the kitchen.

Alex had decided to first go to meet with Adrianna before going to apprehend Father Chris. She wanted to explain the reason associated with taking him back to Cincinnati.

She also wanted to make sure that if help was needed, it would be standing by.

She did not anticipate having a problem but as always she was planning for any contingency.

The Pilot's, preparation to land announcement in El Paso brought her back to current time.

As She and Trey got to the top of the exit ramp, they were greeted by a DEA agent that introduced himself as Fred Smith. He lead them through the restricted area on their way to the luggage area.

He let them know that he would guide them through the process of crossing the border.

He took them to a van that was standing by to take them to the border station. The station was built so that the northern portion was in the US and the southern portion was in Mexico.

Alex looked at Trey and commented that this crossing was much less stressful then the last time.

It was less stressful, but it took much longer. At the station they were introduced by Fred to the Eduardo who had the equivalent Mexican role.

Alex and Trey listened to Eduardo Escobar explain that he would provide transportation and be their escort during their stay in Mexico. He made it clear that they could not make a formal arrest but must convince the person that they were to escort back into the US to come willingly with them.

Alex was not surprised. She just hoped that Father Chris did not know of such a condition.

They would also be driven to any location they desired.

She looked at Trey and commented that at least they did not have to drive.

Alex explained that she needed to first go to Ciudad Victoria where a close friend lived.

When she gave him the specific location she wanted to go to, Eduardo looked at her and commented that the address she had given him was currently occupied by the wife of the former drug cartel boss.

Alex looked back at him and agreed that indeed that was the case but now both she and Adrianna, the widow of that boss, supported charities focused on helping those that needed it.

She added that she planned to extent Adrianna's program to the poor in the US.

Eduardo commented that what he thought was going to be a boring assignment had just gotten very interesting.

He then went on to say that the destination Alex had requested more than doubled the driving time and they would need to determine where they would spend the night.

Alex nodded and said that she wished it wasn't so but that she wanted to make the trip to the compound that day.

They would all stay in Adrianna's compound. She joked that she was sure that they would not need to sleep in the horse barn.

During the drive she listened as Eduardo shared the fact that he had a wonderful wife and three children. His oldest, a son, was just turning twelve. The other two were girls eight and ten years old and as beautiful as their mother. He went on to say that all three were smarter than he.

Alex listened and commented that she hoped to someday meet them to see if indeed they were smarter than their father.

Alex shared that she was called "Aunt" by Trey's son and that indeed he was much smarter than his father.

That brought a chuckle out of Eduardo.

The chatter died down and Alex took in the countryside.

Agriculture was the dominant aspect of the drive until they arrived at Monterrey. The city's industrial and modern appearance was one that any successful city in the US would have.

Highway 85 cut through the heart of the city and Alex was able to take in the bustle and prosperity that was visually evident.

Eduardo confirmed that business in Mexico was doing well. The pay for most workers was still very low but employment was up which meant that the majority of people were better off.

Alex commented that both the Mexican and US economy were supported by those making the least. Equity was not what drove either economy.

She commented that it was greed of the wealthy.

They stopped by a roadside Churrascaria for lunch. One of its specialties was barbecue pork.

Alex's offer to pay was readily accepted. They all declined a Modelo and settled for a soft drink.

Everyone including the driver, who Eduardo had previously introduced as Ricardo sat at a long common table and were served in a family style fashion.

There was more food than the four of them could possibly eat. Alex and Trey both commented on the amount of foot and how delicious it was.

The service was as good as the food and the proprietor kept asking if they wanted more.

All of them put up their hands and said that they could not finish what he had placed on the table.

She left a generous tip and still felt that she had not paid enough.

Alex noted that Ricardo ate very little. As they were getting ready to leave, she spoke to him in Spanish and assured him that he would be able to enjoy one of the most wonderful meals when they got to where they were going.

Eduardo complimented her on her fine control of the Spanish language and that he would not call her a Gringo.

Alex smiled and thanked him for the compliment. She went on to explain that both she and Trey had taken private Spanish lessons since her first trip to Mexico. Their instructor was located in Mexico City, and they took lessons three times a week during their lunch hour.

Eduardo commented that he took English lessons over the internet as well.

Alex joked that she would not call him a wetback since he had such fine control of the American language.

Then Ricardo chimed in and commented that Eduardo did not know how to swim so he would never make it across the Rio Grande into the US and would never be able to use the English he was learning.

Trey piped in that he was a swim instructor and that he would be glad to qualify Eduardo that evening.

Eduardo laughed and replied that he was also a swim instructor and had taught all his kids to be excellent swimmers. He hoped they would never have to go across the Rio Grande, but he hoped they might get accepted into some US university.

The joking back and forth died down and Alex once again closed her eyes and relaxed.

Ricardo turned off Highway 101when Alex pointed to a road that went up the hill. The long narrow road seemed to be taking them into the wilderness.

Suddenly the road widened when it came to a black iron gate. The gate did not open.

An armed guard came around the end column.

He had a shotgun at the ready.

Ricardo rolled down the two windows on his side.

The bright white toothed smile of the guard caught Alex by surprise.

He commented in Spanish that the Black Angel was expected. He gave a wave to the other guard and the gate slowly opened.

Alex smiled back and in Spanish thanked him for his compliment.

<u>*9 Compound*</u>

Alex took in the grand driveway circle with a lush red rose garden in the center.

Eduardo let out a sigh and commented that he was in the wrong line of work and that perhaps he should become a drug lord.

Adrianna, Adolfo and a very good looking lady, and a person that Alex recognized as Maria, stood with her hands on the shoulders of two young girls on each side that were young duplicates of Adriana.

As they hugged, Adrianna whispered in her ear that her daughters did not know how their father had died and that she wanted them to continue to think he had died of a heart attack.

Adrianna took her by the hand and went over to where they were standing and first introduced Maria, the nanny that had been with the family for more than thirty years.

Alex gave her a hug and thanked her for clearing the way into the kitchen.

Maria smile and replied that someone needed to do it.

Alex then gave each of the girls a hug and commented that they were each more beautiful than their mother.

Alex looked at Adrianna and commented that she was looking well.

She then turned to Adolfo.

He introduced Alejandra, a young lady about her size with a radiant smile, sparkling black eyes and a current swept back hair style.

Alex stepped forward and gave her a hug and in Spanish she told her that she had captured the heart of a hero. Alejandra smiled and said that she had indeed, and she was not going to let him go.

Alex then introduced Trey as her work partner and Eduardo as their escort while they were in Mexico.

She pointed to Ricardo and commented that he was starving and that she had promised him the best dinner that he had ever eaten.

Adolfo chuckled and commented that every meal coming from the kitchen was the best that anyone could possible want.

Adrianna suggested that they follow her.

She led them through a long hallway to the back of the house to the pool area.

Alex recognized the cross hallway that she had used to gain access to Ernesto's office. As they exited into the pool area she recognized the veranda where she had followed Adrianna as she was led to the bedroom where there was an escape hatch to the tunnel that led to the woods.

She was somewhat oriented, but she had never seen the house or the ground in daylight. This was the first time she could fill in the details that she had missed in the dark of night. She was impressed with the pure elegance of the house and its exterior.

When Adriana suggested that Adolfo give them a tour of the grounds and the estate Alex commented that she looked forward to it.

The pool area was elevated relative to the rest of the compound. The front of the estate had been raised so that the house and pool area were at the same level but the gardens where at a lower level. Adolfo pointed out that this enriched the grand view of the City below.

Alex commented that it was a grand view and asked how far it was to the city. Adolfo looked at her and smiled, said that it was far enough that it would take a person all night to make the journey. Then he added that he thought it was about sixteen kilometers.

Alex understood his meaning because it had taken her an entire night to walk down the hill with only the star light providing enough light for her to see.

It had been a walk that had ended up at his apartment where he had fed her breakfast and had loaned her his, and Adrianna's old family car.

The tour of the house began upstairs where there were six grand bedrooms. Each was the size of Alex's two bedroom apartment. This time she was able to take in the grandeur and the elegance that the rooms exuded.

The long closets at the back of the rooms were large enough to be apartment suites.

Adolfo commented that he would not be able to show four of the bedrooms because they had been converted to house multiple people and yes even the closets had been converted for family use.

Alex asked if the conversion had to do with the charity work that was now the center of Adrianna's focus.

He replied that indeed it was. He commented that the only flower garden that still remained was the roses in the front of the house. The rest of the ground was covered with greenhouses and outside gardens that grew tomatoes, squash, peppers, and a variety of other food. The fresh vegetables were part of the food distribution network. He added that they included the basics of rice, beans, and canned meat year-round and included fresh food as they had it available.

His farmers were using the latest growing techniques. They rotated their crops in such a fashion that they were always renewing the ground. The green houses utilized hydroponic harvesting of many of their plants. He figured the yields were among the highest in the world.

Alex complimented him on the accomplishment.

Alex was impressed with the work that Adrianna was leading. She especially liked the sign on the side of each of the six parked work trucks that read, "Miracles Powered By Black, White and Latino Angels."

She recognized that they had thought of her when they had made the sign.

Adolfo smiled and said that of course she was thought of since she had made it all possible.

Alex recalled that it had been the message that had linked Adrianna with the five million dollars that had landed in her account.

They heard a bell ringing and Adolfo said that the tour was ending and that they would join everyone that lived in the compound in the newly renovated eating area that housed up to one hundred guests. Today there would only be thirty.

Alex asked if the kitchen had been renovated.

Adolfo replied that the kitchen was exactly as it had been when Ernesto had his heart attack.

Alex smiled and replied that she would like to meet the Chef in the kitchen before dinner.

Adolfo led the group into the kitchen. He introduced everyone. The Chef accepted Alex praise of how everything was kept clean and in order. He asked if she knew any famous Chef's in Cincinnati. She replied that indeed she had one friend that was a Chef at her favorite restaurant and she added that her mother was a non-practicing but certified French trained Chef as well.

She volunteered to introduce him to both of them.

He said that he would look forward to meeting both and asked for their phone numbers so he could do a video call with them.

She took note that the carts were all arranged next to each other and that the cover leading down into the secret tunnel was covered by the carts.

Adrianna introduced Alex as the person who was extending the concept of helping the poor into the US and that Mexican families were one of the top recipients of the help. She pointed out that in the US there were almost an equal number of poor black, white and Hispanics and that Alex's foundation called "Open Hands" served everyone.

The entire gathering stood up and clapped and shouted out "El ángel negro del norte."

Alex smile and in Spanish thanked them for their kind gesture but she wished she could be as good and generous as her hostess, Adrianna.

Shortly after the meal was served, Ricardo commented that the promise that Alex had made was beyond what he had imagined possible. It was one of the best meals he had ever eaten.

Alex replied that he should share that with the Chef.

She watched as Ricardo stood up and walked back into the kitchen.

She laughed when the Chef pushed him out and loudly declared that giving him praise would not get Ricardo any extra food.

Everyone in the room had some sort of comment. And then laughed when another full serving was delivered to Ricardo.

Alex looked at him and commented that he should never pay attention to what was said but to the actions that a person took.

She was soon to have her words echo back at her in a surprising fashion.

10 The No Ears Room

The next morning after breakfast Adrianna led the group into the office where Alex had shot Ernesto between the eyes.

She listened as Adrianna explained that the room had no ears.

Alex felt the past surround her.

Adriana sat down in the chair where Ernesto had sat on the night he had promised to stop his attack on her.

She was standing in the same spot where she had turned to walk away but had heard the click of the gun he had pulled to shoot her in the back.

She had turned and shot him between the eyes.

She was surprised at her reaction.

She stood for a moment and took a deep breath.

She decided to recount that case so that Adrianna and Adolfo and everyone would have the context of what had led her to Ernesto.

She looked around and all the events leading to that moment went through her mind.

It had been two years, but the body count of the trail she had created still went through her mind on almost a daily basis.

She had learned to control her emotions, but she knew that in talking with Trey that she would be dealing with it for years to come and perhaps her lifetime.

He said that he thought that he would never forget his field engagements and the firefights that he had experienced.

She looked at Trey and commented that two years before she and Trey had been abducted by some hoodlums that almost killed him. She had been lucky and had been able to save Trey and learn the name of the person who had ordered that both of them be killed.

She went on to say that Trey had barely survived the brutal beating of being kicked and brutalized while she sat taped to a chair and made to watch.

She had managed to free herself and save both Trey and herself.

She had then chased down every person involved in her and Trey's capture and beating.

The trail to the room they were sitting in was punctuated by fifteen dead bodies, two downed helicopter gunships, a coal barge tug and coal barge and her brand new automobile.

She commented that it was the body count that still haunted her every day.

That trail had led her to the Cartel Chief's mountainside estate and the room where they were now all sitting.

She had confronted him, and he had promised he would end his war with her.

She recalled how as she turned, as if to leave, he had drawn a gun and was raising it to shoot her in the back when she turned and shot him between the eyes and twice in the chest. He was the sixteenth body.

Tears welled up in Adrianna's eyes as she listened to Alex tell of the story that led her to this room the last time she had been in the house.

Adrianna nodded and quietly thanked Alex.

Adolfo did the same.

Alex replied that Adrianna and he had saved her so they should all celebrate that they had found each other.

She then said that she had come back to get their help in capturing an American Catholic priest.

Adrianna wanted to know why a Catholic Priest was the focus of Alex's trip.

She made the point that Adolfo had worked with Alex's analyst that seemed to have access to software that Adolfo said he didn't know existed but that seemed to open every information door to a person's world. So, it seemed that Alex had all the weapons she needed.

Alex stood up and began by saying that her analyst was the part of her team that was constantly saving her.

She shared that he was an old Vietnam veteran, named Johnnie, that she had saved from a local drug distributor who was out to kill him.

He had become an indispensable part of her team.

She said that he was able to hunt down information that others missed.

She added that her previous entry into the compound had been made possible by Johnnie's ability to find the entrance tunnel into the compound.

He had been the one who pointed out that the leader of the Gulf cartel had been the one that owned the gunship helicopters that had attacked her.

Her determination to end the attacks had inspired Johnnie to not only find out who and where that person was located but had also found out how to get into the place.

He had also uncovered the early history of how Adrianna had come to marry the person responsible for her father's death.

With Johnnie's help and with the DEA facilitating getting her armed in Mexico she made the trip that led to Ernesto's heart attack.

Alex continued and said that she had been certain that a mole existed in the police department who had been responsible for sharing information with the cartel, and she had Johnnie search for such a person.

They found him but before she could arrest him, he was eliminated by a cartel assassin. She shared that she had eliminated the assassin after her return from Mexico.

Alex made the point that every one of the final count of seventeen fatalities had the chance to surrender and be arrested.

They had instead all chosen to try to shoot her.

Their choices had all been mistakes that cost them their lives.

She shared that on the night she faced Ernesto she had expected to die afterwards.

Adrianna had entered and led her from the room and guided her to a secret ladder that was in the bedroom closet that led down to the cave where she had first entered the estate.

She had made her way down the mountain to the door that Adolfo opened. He had provided her transportation that got her to the US border.

This was her first visit where she had been able to see the estate in the light of day.

Alex stopped and looked around.

There was silence in the room.

Trey broke the silence and commented that there was very little luck associated with that case.

He went on to say that Alex's tenacious actions and her tremendous skill made all the difference.

He was in a coma in the hospital for that entire time.

Johnnie had become her back up in the States but she had come to Mexico alone

She had acted in a manner that caused him great concern for her safety but one that had changed his life for the better.

Alex asked Trey to explain the current trip's purpose and sat down next to Adrianna.

She noticed the tears in Adrianna's eyes.

She reached over and put her hand on Adrianna's and squeezed her hand and quietly thanked her.

Trey described the situation that Father Chris, now going by the title Father Jones, had skipped on a summons to appear in front of the Grand Jury. He and Alex were to escort him back to Cincinnati and ensure that he made his appearance.

Eduardo then ask what specifically was the Father going to be in front of a Grand Jury for.

Trey looked at Alex.

She looked around the room and replied that he had exploited his influence with some Altar boys.

Adolfo stood up and commented that Father Jones was now working with children in his current station at the Church in Monterrey.

Trey replied that they had learned that the previous Friday and that by Monday evening they had arrived in Mexico and traveled to Adrianna's estate.

The two of them had the same anxiety that Adolfo had.

Eduardo said that they needed to get to Father Jones before he was exposed and a mob took action.

He would make sure Father Jones understood that if he did not accept traveling back to Cincinnati, his life would quickly end in a Mexican prison when the word got out that he was a pedophile.

Adrianna stood up and commented that she now understood why Alex had not said anything in detail about this situation. She suggested that Adolfo be added to the team that was going back to Monterrey.

Eduardo commented that he could not agree to that participation, but that Adolfo could follow in one of the trucks to deliver food for the hungry. If he happened to be needed he would be close by.

Alex thanked Adrianna and agreed that delivering food for the hungry in Monterrey would be a good idea. She asked whether a truck could be ready to go immediately. She needed to get back to Monterrey as soon as possible. She wanted to have Father Chris on the way to the border by late afternoon.

Eduardo stood up and declared he was ready to leave.

Adolfo said he had a loaded truck and was ready to follow.

Alex looked at Trey and commented that it would be hard to control such an eager group but that she was sure it was the right group.

How right that statement would be when the action in Monterrey furiously exploded.

11 Monterrey

Alex stood and led the way out of the room. She was now anxious to get to Monterrey and "Invite" Father Chris to travel with her back into the US.

Sharing the story of how she had ended up in the room with no ears the first time had seemed like a heavy load had lifted from her soul.

Adriana had hugged her again as they left the room and said that she would be forever in her debt.

Alex said that there was no debt there was only a lifelong friendship.

Adolfo broke off and said he was pulling the truck out front and would follow them.

Alex nodded and asked if his cell phone was charged and that she planned to organize the team as they drove, and she would include him in the planning.

She looked to Eduardo and asked him to inform Ricardo to stay at the speed limit. She knew they were all in a rush, but she did not want to get any local police mixed up in the apprehension of Father Jones.

She spent some time in the car in discussion with Trey. They decided on first checking to see if Father Chris was in his apartment. Then they would follow his walking route and finally they would go to the church.

They contacted Adolfo and shared their plan. He suggested that he would begin food distribution in the park across from the Cathedral but at the other end of the park. He would then stand by and wait to see what happened. He said that if Alex found Father Chris and had him in her car, his role would be to go back to the compound and call it a day. He said that it would be better if it happen that way.

Alex agreed and thanked him for his help.

She then asked Ricardo if there was a radio station that played Mexican Mariachi music. She spent the rest of the ride thinking through each of the various scenarios she might face.

The music served to let her focus on what she was thinking.

The arrival to Father Chris' apartment put Alex at full vigilance. They entered the building and located the apartment.

Alex called out as if she were a friend coming to visit. There was no answer.

She then quickly picked the door lock.

Eduardo raised his eyebrow and commented that all he saw was a key opening the door.

There was no one inside.

They did not see Father Chris as they drove around the park.

Alex asked Ricardo to drop them off in front of the Church and then drive the car to the back of the church. He nodded, smiled, and added, "It is a Cathedral."

Alex smiled and repeated what he said and added "and a very beautiful one" in her best Spanish. She understood the message that he was conveying.

She led the way up the stairs into the entrance. The entrance doors were massive ten foot high and at least three inches thick with intricately carved biblical scenes. It opened smoothly but Alex could feel it's massive weigh.

Alex made sure that both Trey and Eduardo understood that there were to be no guns used in the Cathedral and watched as they each nodded understanding.

She then took the main isle.

Eduardo took the left side at the other end of the pews.

Trey took the right.

She slowly paced up the aisle. At each step she would look to her left and then to the right. She knew that she was in an adrenalin state when she realized that she felt that she was creeping up an unusually long Nave.

She reached the front row and looked at Eduardo. She immediately dropped to the floor when she saw the look on his face.

She heard Trey shout a warning at as she rolled between the pews to her right.

The ax head at the end of a long ceremonious handle wedged into the side of the end of the pew. The sound it made as it contacted the end of the pew let Alex know that it had been swung with high intensity.

Father Chris was on the other end of the handle.

He had been surprised to see who had come in the door and was in a rage and intent on killing the person he knew was from Cincinnati.

Alex immediately launched her body over the pew as if she were going over backward over a pole vault. She had her belt knife in her hand as she landed. She shouted out, "Don't shoot, Don't shoot" and buried the knife into Father Chris's thigh with all her might and then she jumped up on the alter surface.

As he dropped down she hit him in the neck with a hand chop and watched his eyes roll as he passed out.

She felt for Father Chris's vitals. She had tried not to hit him too hard. The blow she had delivered was one that could be used to kill someone.

Trey and Eduardo were immediately at her side.

Her phone buzzed and she listened to Adolfo warn her that the word had somehow gone out that Father Chris was molesting children and that almost everyone in the park was headed for the Cathedral.

Alex then took notice of the shouts coming from the park.

Adolfo had instructed his driver to go around the back of the Cathedral.

Alex looked at Eduardo and told him to hold back the crowd and that in three minutes he could tell them that the Cathedral was empty, and that Father Chris was not there. He could then let them in to see for themselves.

She was surprised at the amount of blood on the floor. Trey had used his belt as a tourniquet and had stopped the bleeding and was now beginning to drag Father Chris toward the back door.

Alex got the ax loose from the pew and put it back in the holder that was next to the Altar. She looked around for a way to wipe up the blood. The pure white Altar cloth was the only thing in sight.

She watched as Adolfo came in and helped Trey carry Father Chris out.

She carefully wiped up the blood and then stopped long enough to light a Votive candle and ask for forgiveness and for help in getting away.

She was at the rear door when she heard Eduardo say that everyone could go in and see for themselves that Father Jones was not inside.

Alex jumped into the truck and as the doors slammed shut, she was glad that there were internal lights.

She looked toward the front where a small window into the cab opened as she heard Adolfo explain that they were slowly leaving the area.

He let her know that Eduardo had called him and had said he was clear of the area and knew that they were all heading back to the compound.

Father Chris came to. He slowly realized he was in the back of a truck. He then saw the person who he had tried to kill. He cursed her and said that she would go to hell for what she had done.

Alex smiled at him and replied if that was where she ended up then they would see each other again. She went on to say that on the other hand it had been a hand from above that had saved her so she might not have to visit him after all.

Trey told Father Chris to shut up and pray that he did not lose his leg because the tourniquet was going to be on it for almost four hours.

Alex asked Adolfo if there was someone at the compound that could take care of Father Jones' leg wound.

He said that they had such a person.

When they arrived at the compound the person that came into the truck instructed everyone to step aside and that he would take care of the situation with his personal assistants.

Alex stood outside of the van.

She was now surrounded by many of the residents.

Adrianna looked at her and commented to her that even without a gun she was deadly.

Alex complimented her on having a doctor as a resident of the complex.

Adrianna chuckled and replied that he was their veterinarian and one of the few on her payroll.

He said that he would work on this animal that called himself a priest but only because he was to be escorted back to the US to stand trial.

It was sometime later that Alex watched as Father Chris was put on a flatbed wheelbarrow and moved into what was now a barn where the cows were milked.

Adrianna explained that the barn was the only place where her flock had agreed she could put Father Chris.

Alex gave short laugh and commented that her flock had the right idea.

It was late but Alex asked if her team could get a light snack and then get some sleep.

Not long after she was in bed. It was pitch black when the hand on her shoulder caused an immediate defensive reaction. She was on her feet ready to defend herself.

Adrianna had jumped back and had her hands up in front of her.

She apologized for having touched her and would remember to use her voice in the future.

She said that word had somehow gone out that Father Jones was at the compound.

She had come to let her know that a mob was coming up from the 101 and approaching the compound.

Adrianna had asked that Father Jones be removed from the compound so that she could tell the mob that he was not in the compound.

Alex followed Adolfo as he wheeled a complaining Father Chris on the flatbed wheelbarrow. Adolfo had a helper who was walking ahead with a rope around his waist pulling.

Trey was carrying a backpack that the chef had prepared for them as a morning meal.

The chef had wished Alex a safe journey out of Mexico and commented that he hoped she would accept Adolfo's wedding invitation that she would receive in the near future. She would then see just how delicious his meals could be.

Alex had thanked him.

She was now reliving the trip she had made down the same trail guided only by the light of the moon.

This time she had the luxury of company and the use of a flashlight.

She and Trey were in back. He commented on the beauty of the trail.

Alex replied that she agreed but that when she had made her last trip down the hill she had not been able to enjoy it. She had to make her way in the dark and she had been worried about pursuit.

As they reached the bottom where Alex remembered having to go over a stone wall.

Adolfo pointed out the car.

Alex was surprised to see Eduardo and Ricardo standing beside the car. She wondered how they had gotten past the mob and out of the compound and down the long lane that came up the highway.

Eduardo explained that Adrianna had explained to the crowd that Father Jones was not in the compound. After some of the crowds leaders had checked out her claim she invited them in for an early breakfast and escorted them into the cafeteria.

He and Ricardo had then simply driven the car, that they had backed into the garage, out of the garage and down to the101. There was no one outside because they were all inside enjoying one of the chef's breakfast.

Alex gave a small chuckle and commented that Adrianna knew how to handle a crowd.

11 Monterrey

12 El Paso

Bill was frustrated.

He had been relieved when Alex asked he and Travis to focus on the money trial. He figured that it would be the easier and less emotional part of the two cases.

He and Travis had interviewed everyone that John had on his list of people associated that might contest the deceased wife's half of the couples combined wealth into a trust managed by her husband.

He was told by John that it was a friendly divorce where the two had remained friends but that each had agreed that they were seeking a different path at this point in their lives.

Bill didn't exactly understand such a relationship, but he figured that it was better than the bitter divorce fights that several acquaintances had gone through.

He knew Trevor was frustrated as he, because he was eating two donuts each morning as he strummed the keys on his computer.

They both cornered Johnnie and asked if he was making any progress.

Bill said that they wanted the miracle that he always provided to Alex.

Johnnie shook his head and replied that no he had not figured out who was behind the lawsuit to block the husband from being the trustee of the Trust. He also had not found the people that were after the money. He made the point that Alex always seemed to trigger some off the wall idea that guided him into a new search routine. He commented that he had not wanted to call her while she was in Mexico.

He wanted her to concentrate on finding and bringing Father Chris back to Cincinnati.

Bill saw the Chief waving him over.

He nudged Trevor and the two of them walked into the Chief's office.

The Chief asked whether there was any new leads in the money case.

Bill replied that they were empty handed and not sure what to do next.

The Chief made the comment that they all needed Alex to come back and use her intuition to find the breakthrough in the money case.

He went on to say that he had received a call from Alex. She was on the way to El Paso. She had Father Chris with her, and he was planning to sue the department for being mistreated.

She explained that he had tried to kill her, and she had taken him down and yes she stabbed him with a bowie knife and hit him with her hand.

Trevor commented that the Father should be glad to be alive. He added that he did not know that Alex carried a bowie knife and she had small hands. He said that the fact that the Father was still alive meant that he should be thanking Alex.

The Chief went on to say that Alex planned to be at the border by late afternoon and would bring Father Chris with her.

The Chief then let Bill and Trevor know that he wanted them to meet Alex at the border, take Father Chris into their custody and bring him back to Cincinnati.

He handed Bill the itinerary that put he and Trevor on a plane within the hour.

The Chief then instructed Bill to let Alex know that she had done a great job but was relieved and would not be on the case until she reported back to the station.

He was also to tell her that she should stop by in Chicago and visit family or just take it easy for a couple of days.

Bill walked out of the office, cleared his desk, and let Johnnie know that Alex was on her way back with Father Chris.

He suggested that Johnnie call her in the evening after she was back in the states.

The two of them grabbed their stuff from the locker room.

They took a taxi to the airport and had to run to where their plane was waiting for them.

The flight attendant was waiting to escort them on.

She told them that not only had the pilot been holding the plane but two passengers each made five hundred dollars for giving up their seats for a later flight.

The other passengers clapped as they got on and took their seats.

Bill gave everyone a salute and sat down to catch his breath.

They had a connection flight in San Antonio where they were met by the ticket agent and escorted to a plane that would take them to El Paso.

The agent commented that somebody was pulling strings to get them through the terminal because having an escort was not a normal service.

When they arrived in El Paso, they were surprised to be met by a DEA agent. He greeted them and told them he was to take them to the location where Alex, Trey and Father Chris would enter the US.

Bill was intrigued by the fact that there was a building that was half in Mexico and half in the US. The DEA agent commented that there were several similar arrangements along both the Mexican and the Canadian border. They were used only for situations similar to the that they were involved in.

They were guided to the room where Alex, Trey and Father Chris would be escorted in by the Mexican equivalent of the DEA.

He explained that Alex and Trey had been escorted the entire time they had been in Mexico.

Bill looked at Trevor and commented that he wondered how Alex had convinced Father Chris to voluntarily cross back into the US where he would be in jail until he went before the Grand Jury.

Bill really enjoyed the surprised look on Alex's face when she walked into the room.

For once he appreciated Trevor's comment about the fact that the Chief wanted Father Chris to stay alive and had asked the better team to take him away from the dangerous person that was bringing him back into the US.

Alex replied to Trevor's line by replying that the Chief must have seen Trevor spending too much time in the coffee break area and figured he needed to put him to work.

Bill chuckled and commented that it indeed Trevor was eating two donuts a day and the Chief was trying to save his life.

He then asked how she had gotten Father Chris to agree to return.

Alex introduced Eduardo who had been a great escort and who had offered Father John, as Father Chris was known in Mexico, the alternative of spending a few remaining days alive in a Mexican prison. After a few days he had assured Father John that his head would be displayed on a pike and seen in newscasts.

Bill shook Eduardo's hand and said that he wished that Father Chris had taken him up on his offer to stay in Mexico.

He then asked if Father Chris was officially in the US.

He was given a signed document that stated that Father Christopher Jones was voluntarily accompanying Alex Evercrest and Trey McGregor into the US.

When it was confirmed that he was indeed in the US, Bill officially arrested him and put him in handcuffs.

He listened as Father Chris objected and said that as a priest, he should not have to be handcuffed.

Bill chuckled and said he knew of no special privilege for a priest and that Father Chris could lodge a complaint when he got in front of a judge.

He then passed on the Chief's praise for the good work that the two of them had done. The Chief said that he had gotten a lot of praise about the good work from someone that simply said that she was the Angel on the hill.

He conveyed the message that Alex should consider going fishing and that she and Trey had the rest of the week off.

He was pleased to see Alex smile and say that she thought going fishing was a good idea.

Trey said that he wanted a quiet weekend and that he planned to grill hamburgers and dogs in his back yard and take it easy.

Bill made a comment that he and Trevor were waiting for a miracle from her analyst and that that this analyst was needing her inspiration.

Alex nodded and said that she thought maybe she would see if Trey would grill her a brat and share a cold one over the weekend. This would let her travel to Cincinnati and work with Johnnie.

Her unconventional approach would once again spark an idea that would lead Johnnie to find the money footsteps that he was seeking.

13 Breakthrough

Johnnie had celebrated when he had located Father Chris in Mexico. Alex's contact in Mexico had helped him pinpoint the city and the Cathedral in which Father Chris was active.

Alex had achieved the goal of getting Father Chris back to the US.

He on the other hand, was still on step one of trying to find the person who was contesting the financial arrangements that were the focus of the second case.

The money case that he thought would be an easier one was proving to be very elusive and significantly more difficult than he had anticipated.

He had resisted calling Alex while she was in Mexico.

When Bill came out of the Chief's office they let him know they were rushing to the airport to catch a flight to El Paso to relieve Alex of her "guest."

They had suggested that he call her either later in the day or next morning and see if she might find a new way of tracking down who was making the move to gain control of the divorce settlement.

Johnnie decided on the next morning. He would take a breather and see if some new idea would surface.

He was sure that Alex, as always, would trigger a new idea. She had the knack of asking what she called off the wall questions and suggesting off the wall ideas.

He was just wrapping up and about to walk out to his bike when he answered his phone and heard Alex's voice.

He immediately felt better.

He chuckled when she said that if he would provide her breakfast of two pancakes covered in plenty of syrup and topped with two over easy eggs, bacon on the side and a hot cup of coffee they could tackle the problem together on the following morning.

Johnnie readily agreed. He got up and let the Chief know that Alex planned to return to Cincinnati and that he would be working with her on the money case.

He joked with the Chief that Alex said that the fish he had caught on the department fishing outing and was now up behind his desk was so large that it discouraged her from fishing.

That brought a laugh from the Chief.

He replied that Alex was probably waiting until she had someone shooting at her when she fished so that it would be more exciting.

Johnnie hummed a song as he rode his bicycle slowly back to his apartment.

The next morning when there was a knock on his apartment door he had Alex's breakfast order on the table.

He opened the door and accepted her good morning and a hug. He led her to the table and sat down across from her.

He asked about her Mexico adventure and listened as she filled him in on the details.

At the end he complimented her on only stabbing and not shooting Father Chris between the eyes.

He laughed when she said she almost did shoot him but realized she was in Church and should act in a more subdued manner so she only used her knife and hit him with the best karate shot to the neck that she could muster.

He then went into the money case and shared that determining who was behind trying to gain control of the millions, that had been put into the trust, was proving harder than tracking Father Chris.

He said it had to be someone that was distant because nothing linked to any correspondence that had occurred in the last few years.

Alex sat and listened as she ate her breakfast. She periodically asked a clarification question but concentrated on what Johnnie was explaining.

After he had finished she asked for another coffee and suggested that Johnnie have his breakfast.

As he poured the coffee he let her know that he had eaten his breakfast before her arrival. He had anticipated that she would listen as he talked.

He asked if she had any ideas.

Alex nodded and asked if he had thoroughly traced the people associated with the husband.

Johnnie replied that he had done all the close relationships and found nothing unusual.

Alex then asked if Johnnie could find out who might be a client of Samuel Ellington III and have some family connection with the husband.

Johnnie smiled and said he thought he could do that, but he would need access to the NSA software that was only available from the departments connection from the station.

Alex nodded and said that she would get her bike and they could ride in together. She knew she would hear from the Chief and certainly get a ribbing from Trevor, but she wanted to clear the deck on this case as soon as possible.

Once they were in the office, Johnnie watched and listened as Alex was ribbed by Trevor about coming into work instead of taking Bill's advice to go fishing.

He followed Alex into the Chief's office and laughed as she reinforced his earlier joke about the mounted fish behind the desk discouraging her from her fishing trip.

He listened as she negotiated getting the time off that the Chief had offered after Johnnie delivered his second analysis miracle.

Johnnie hung his head and apologized for having taken so long but that Alex had cracked the whip and put him back on the trail.

He relaxed when the Chief complained about his lack of influence over his hired help and that if Alex wanted he would take down the fish so that she could once again be inspired to go fishing.

There was a moment of silence.

Johnnie almost laughed when the Chief asked the name of the restaurant that Alex had promised to take him if he delivered his miracle.

It was clear to him that the Chief was pleased with Alex's dedication and that he knew his people well.

He nodded as the Chief told them to quit talking and go do some real work.

As Alex led the way to their usual work room, he commented that she had done a good job training the Chief.

He laughed when she replied that the Chief had not yet agreed to let her have the day off in the future.

She was now working and that he had better deliver his miracle otherwise she would not be able to go fishing.

Johnnie connected to the NSA software and began to utilize its power to check into the clients of Samuel Ellington III.

The name Lucas Walker, a Cincinnati council member came up.

Johnnie commented that Lucas Walker was not related to Fionna Maninsky, but he had somehow decided that he should intervene.

It seemed unlikely that he would be able to gain control of the money but for some reason he was pushing to get someone to contest the way the money was to be managed.

Alex commented that she doubted that he would be the one that would take such direct action. She bet that if he was involved it would be indirectly.

Johnnie decided to see if Lucas Walker was active on any social media. He found several negative comments about the fact that the divorce settlement had named Walter Maninsky as the proprietor of Fiona Maninsky's Charity Remainder Trust.

Johnnie then reviewed the people that were on the social media distribution.

He quietly said Bingo.

He had the name of the person that would be the legal challenger.

The person was a distant cousin.

Richard William Cutter was what his name implied. He was a rough and tough lumberman residing in northern Idaho.

Johnnie did a little more digging and found that Richard was a heavy drinker and had been arrested three times for driving under the influence.

He was thirty nine, single but had two kids by two separate women.

There was one last piece of information was a jewel that John and Alex would both love.

Richard was in Cincinnati not more than two blocks from the station. He lowered the lid to his laptop, smiled, looked at Alex, said he wanted to eat ribs, enjoy the view and see logs float down the river.

Alex smiled and said, "don't play me, give me the miracle.

He quickly saved his information. He looked at her and said that he would divulge the information after lunch.

Johnnie went on to tease that he had the name of the person and his location in Cincinnati.

When asked by Alex who the person was, Johnnie smiled and said that he would eat first, enjoy desert, with a glass of Moscato as he watched the logs float down the river.

Alex smiled and responded that if Johnnie was that sure then she was inviting the whole team to join them for a victory lunch.

<u>*14 The River View*</u>

Alex had invited everyone associated with the two cases to Johnnie's victory lunch. She promised that he would let them all know who was behind trying to get control of the millions of dollars that was now in trust.

She looked at the Chief and asked if it could be considered a business lunch.

The Chief complained loudly about such a lunch and that it would put a huge dent in his budget.

He groaned loudly and nodded his head but made the point that any alcohol would be paid for separately.

He went on to say that those drinking would need to take the rest of the day off.

Alex laughed and said she would stand for the drinks but anyone drinking more than three had to take a taxi home.

She called John and asked if he would like to join the detective unit for lunch. He would find out who the person that could legally challenge the person who would be the executor of the trust.

She went on to suggest that he would then be able to direct the team on the next steps.

The Chief pulled her aside and asked what she had done to facilitated the breakthrough.

She smiled and said that she had insisted that Johnnie make her a pancake and syrup breakfast and tell her about the work he had done.

She went on to say that the syrup gave her a sugar high, and she then began to sing.

Johnnie had put up his hands and asked her to stop and that he would figure out who was behind the grab for control of the trust.

She watched as the Chief looked down to the floor and then looked at her and asked if she had a clue how the breakthrough happened.

Alex smiled and said she didn't even know what the breakthrough was, and that Johnnie was using it as leverage so he could have ribs, wine, and watch logs float down the river.

The Chief chuckled and commented that she had set up a con artist as a department analyst.

At lunch they all gathered at the restaurant and were seated so all of them had a view of the river. It was a set menu of ribs unless someone was vegetarian.

And no one was.

The bibs were passed out and everyone was ready to enjoy ribs with plenty of sauce on them.

They all listened as Johnnie complained about the fact that he had not seen one log floating down the river.

Everyone on the team asked about what he had discovered.

Alex enjoyed the fact that he would deflect the questions with a rib bone or one of the eating utensils and make a superfluous comment.

She knew Johnnie was taking a victory lap and enjoying it. He had been extremely frustrated, and the breakthrough must have been significant because he had immediately bargained for the lunch.

She told him that he had been accused of being a con artist.

Johnnie replied that he was more like the pied piper and was being cautious and taking his payment up front.

Desert arrived and soon Johnnie was done with his apple pie and ice cream and was reaching for his third glass of Moscato when Alex loudly said he had to divulge his information if he wanted to take another sip.

She enjoyed Johnnie's comment about the fact that it had been one of the best meals he had ever eaten.

He then went on to explain that Samuel Ellington III was working with councilman, William Langley, a city councilman on the case because Langley felt that having the trust managed by Walter Maninsky was not appropriate.

William had found a distant cousin of the wife that was a lumberjack in northern Idaho who had agreed to challenge the right of the husband in the management of the trust.

William Langley had made an agreement with Richard Cutter, the cousin of the deceased Fiona Maninsky to lodge the complaint and to seek to be the executor of the trust.

Johnnie went on to say that there was no mention of any money exchange, but he made the point that the cousin was a laborer in the logging industry.

He went on to say that he had checked him out and that he was a roughhouse kind of guy that lived paycheck to paycheck. He was a heavy drinker and had been arrested three times for driving under the influence.

Johnnie said he was sure that when they got to see the paperwork they would find Langley's or Samuel Ellington III's name involved in helping to manage the trust.

He made the point that the cousin would most likely get drinking money and Langley and Ellington would end up sharing the income from the money in the trust.

Alex had watched John's face as Johnnie shared what he had found out.

John was nodding and agreeing with what Johnnie was saying.

She smiled when John offered to give Johnnie a huge bonus and probably double his salary if he would work for him. He commented that he was sure he had paid that much to several agencies and had nothing to show for it.

Johnnie thanked him for the offer but replied that his current boss gave him hugs, kisses and took him out to eat ribs and that he just could not see John being able to fill in that role.

Johnnie stopped and pointed out to the river to a log floating by. He commented that it was just like his breakthrough on the case, just as he was about to give up on the case the information magically appeared.

And then he grinned and said that he had one more surprise.

Johnnie used his fingers to do a drum roll on the edge of the table.

He then in almost a whisper said, "Richard Cutter is staying in a hotel on the Cincinnati square."

John looked at Johnnie and simply said that he now understood why Alex called him her miracle worker.

Alex then raised her glass of Pellegrino and made a toast to the analyst that always delivered miracles.

She laughed when Johnnie said she owned him a tray of her cookies and a breakfast at his favorite restaurant.

Trey closed the conversation with the question of what restaurant was not one of Johnnie's favorites.

Lunch had taken almost two hours. She looked at the Chief and asked if he really wanted a sleepy, inebriated set of detectives back in the office.

The Chief replied that he was going home. Everyone could do as they pleased.

On the way out John stopped her and asked how she had such overwhelming support of everyone that worked with her.

He wanted to know her secret.

She smiled and said that she followed her mother's advice to, "treat everyone the way you wish to be treated because everything comes back around."

She said that it had served her well and it took no effort.

John then asked if there was any chance that she would go with him if he could set up an interview with Richard Cutter.

Alex said she would love to meet Richard and show him the error of is way.

She would do much more. She would show Richard a better way to live his life.

15 Don't Shoot

*H*anna sat nervously as she waited for Alex to arrive. When John had suggested she take Father Chris's case she had been apprehensive.

She was sure her gender would be an additional hurtle to overcome when in court in front of a jury. She wondered why he was giving her the better of the two cases and later learned his reason.

Her relationship with John had been on an uphill journey in a slow but steady pace. She was eager for the case against Father Chris to be over. She knew it was one of the barriers to her going to the next level with John.

She knew that John was keeping himself as far from the case as possible.

He was also being conservative in dating her.

She figured her relationship would be back on a normal pace once the case was over.

She worried about getting the required seventy five percent of the Grand Jury to agree with her prosecutor that Father Chris's actions warranted an indictment.

She had a top prosecutor who felt that they had a shot at getting Father Chris to be indicted and then go in front of a jury of his peers, but he made the point that a pedophile priest might get a break.

He had gone on to say if the Grand Jury did not support the case, he would still charge Father Chris. He made the point that the support of the Grand Jury would help their case in the regular court and the regular trial would begin sooner because he would not have to convince a judge that a trial was warranted.

She wondered if the Grand Jury would listen to and believe her two witnesses?

They seemed to be reluctant to speak forcefully against Father Chris.

It was almost as if they were still under the influence of Father Chris.

She wished she had strong and forceful witnesses. She continued coaching and rehearsing them. She was determined to get the case heard and to get the votes she needed.

She had been surprised when Alex asked for a meeting. She had mentioned that she might have pertinent information for the case.

Hanna did not know what information would make a difference.

She had been impressed that Alex had been able to locate and bring Father Chris back to the US when the three agencies that she had paid a ton of money to had come up empty handed.

She was now hoping that the information that Alex mentioned would be of help.

The knock on her office door came as a relief. She let out the breath she seemed to have been holding and said, "come in." She stood up and went around the desk.

The bright white smile on Alex's face immediately made her feel better. The cup of coffee that she extended in greeting put the dot at the end of the sentence.

She thought to herself, "much better."

After Alex put the cup down on the desk she turned and accepted Hanna's hand but pulled her in and gave her a hug.

Alex asked how the day was going and listened as Hanna shared her concerns about her witnesses and the fact that the two seemed to be on the timid side.

Alex asked if after she shared her information there might be an opportunity for her to work with the two witnesses.

Hanna was drawn out by Alex's seeming relaxed and very interested expression. She now understood John's comment that Alex had drawn more out of him about his experience than he had ever shared with anyone.

She said that the two were in the next room listening to her instructions and she would arrange for Alex to spend some time with them.

She took a sip of her coffee and then she looked at Alex and asked what she wanted to cover.

She responded to Alex's request to be educated on the Grand Jury process. She clarified that it would only be the prosecutor and the grand jury in the room. Each supporting witness would be brought in separately and share their information with the jury. The last witness if they chose to be present would be the person being accused of a potential crime.

She went on to explain that afterwards the Grand Jury would deliberate and determine whether charges were warranted. The prosecutor then had the discretion as to whether to bring charges against the accused. If the prosecutor brought charges, the case would move forward to where a Judge, Jury, the defendant, and the defense lawyer were present in the same common court. It was in that court were guilt or innocence would be determined. The sentencing if guilty was the verdict, was then a separate sentencing session.

Alex thanked her for the explanation. She went on to say that she had information in the form of a formal document, and several video clips that might be of help. The evidence was not about the charge of pedophilia, but a separated charge and she did not know when the charges would be pertinent.

Hanna reached out her hand as Alex held out the papers and a SD card. She was pleased to hear that the information had a secure chain of evidence that had remained secure and had been handled exactly as it would have been with any crime scene evidence.

Hanna reviewed the document of an Eduardo Garcia that stated that he had been present when Father Chris, known in Mexico as Father Jones had agreed voluntarily to be escorted back to the US by an Alex Evercrest and Trey McGregor the two members of the Cincinnati Unit. He verified that he had been with and escorted Alex and Trey the entire time they had been in Mexico.

She then reviewed the corresponding document that showed that Father Chris had agreed to be escorted back to Cincinnati by a Bill Danson and his partner Travis Carter.

Her phone did not have a slot to play an SD card, so she called her support and asked if there was such a device in the office. She smiled when she heard that it was one of her support's tool that was always available.

She looked at Alex and commented that she had already made the day much brighter and asked what she would see on the video.

When Alex shared that it was of Father Chris as he tried to kill her and why she had wounded and incapacitated him, Hanna held her breath.

Her case had just been greatly enhanced.

The card reader was delivered, and Hanna plugged in the SD card and almost immediately reacted to the scene of an axe descending toward Alex's head and miraculously missing as Axel launched herself between the pews. She could see Father Chris trying to free the ax head from where it was lodged in wood at the end of the Pew.

Then in what seemed an impossible move she witnessed Alex vault the back of the pew like a pole vaulter and as she was going over pulling something from her waist and then burying the small blade into Father Chris's leg and immediately jumping up to strike him on the side of the neck.

She also heard Alex's voice loudly shouting, "don't shoot, don't shoot."

Father Chris fell momentarily out of view but almost immediately the video captured Alex checking his vitals.

Then the video stopped.

Hanna looked across to Alex and commented that she did not believe such action was humanly possible.

The video would mean that Father Chris would also be charged with attempted murder of a police officer.

Hanna asked Alex why she had chosen to use a knife instead her weapon with which she was known to be an expert.

She liked Alex's reply that they were in church, and she had reminded her two backups that they should not use their weapons.

Hanna called the prosecutor and asked if she could arrange a meeting prior to the Grand Jury session.

She told him that she had evidence that would seal Father Chris's case.

She asked if Alex was up to having lunch with her. She was disappointed when Alex declined and said that she was going for a long run right after she spent a few moments with the two pedophile victims. She asked that they be brought into Hanna's office and get to see the video that Hanna had just seen.

The two witnesses came in and Alex introduced herself and said that she wanted to break the spell that Father Chris might have over them. She said that his behavior was not acceptable and he was personally a thief, a person willing to kill someone as well as a pedophile.

She showed the video and could see that it had a positive impact. She then shared the fact that he had also taken several million dollars from the church.

She then added that she knew of a very successful person that had also been a victim of Father Chris.

This person had spent years overcoming the negative impact that Father Chris had on him. She then asked the two if they were willing to make sure Father Chris would never again be able to do to some other boy what he had done to them.

They both agreed that it was what they wanted to do.

Alex said that they had to step up and convince the Grand Jury to recommend a criminal trial.

They would only do that if they could stand in front of them and project strength, to be clear in the way they described their feelings and to look all the jury members in the eyes and ask three simple questions.

What would you have done?

What would you want your child to do?

What as juror are you now going to do to stop it from happening again?

She emphasized that they should look out directly straight at the jurors.

She asked whether they could do that.'

When they both yes, she said they should practice with each other every day until the day they appeared in front of the jury. She made the point that each of them would be standing alone but she would be outside waiting to congratulate them.

Hanna was impressed with what in just a few minutes Alex had done for her case.

She needed to decompress.

She had been delivered a winning hand.

She went to John's office so she could show him the video and tell him about the impact that Alex had on her two witnesses.

She knew he would be as overwhelmed as she was.

It was hard to keep from shouting and jumping up and down as if she had just scored the winning point in a basketball game.

16 The Cutter

Cincinnati was turning out to be an interesting place. He had taken a walk along the River Front Park and sat watching the river flow past the serpentine wall.

Cutter as he liked to be called, had already enjoyed one night of visiting the downtown bars and had enjoyed several good meals. He would never have been able to afford to be doing what he was now about, but he had been given a nice piece of cash advance on the millions that he had been assured would soon come to be under his control.

His hotel had been paid for.

This was the life. He hoped that he could stop working and just enjoy living the good life.

He actually disliked the lawyer who was the biggest egotist that he had ever experienced. He even wondered whether he could be trusted. He told himself not to sign anything until he found another lawyer he could trust.

The councilman was easier to get along with, but Cutter wondered why he had such a passion to remove Walter Maninsky from the trust.

Even if he didn't care, he planned to find out. It was all adding up to be some sort of a con.

It seemed to him that neither of them had any reason to challenge to get control of is distant cousin's money, but he was sure if that control came his way they would want to share the spoils.

He figured the councilman's reason was due to some kind of long time rivalry.

Cutter could identify with that since there were a couple of guys from high school that he hated only because they had competed for the same position in football or in getting dates.

He was sitting in the lounge bar as a table watching a basketball game when he was approached by a well-dressed white guy and a good looking Black lady.

The white guy introduced himself as John Williams and then introduce the woman as Alex Evercrest.

He had no clue who John Williams was, but he immediately knew Alex.

He had followed all the news reports about her and was impressed with her record and her ability to out gun the folks shooting at her.

He stood up and was immediately aware that his six foot six height and his huge body size made her look like a midget.

He was almost twice her height.

He shook her hand and said that he had seen her on the news several times and that her moniker of being "Cincinnati's Black Annie Oakley" really impressed him.

He went on to say that he thought he might be a better shot and it was too bad that they couldn't see if he was right.

He listened as she replied that if he would listen for about half an hour to what John was about to share with him she would arrange for them to be at a target range so that he would know just how good he was.

Cutter looked at her and knew he was going to listen.

He like her direct confident nature.

He was sure he would embarrass her but hey, "that was life."

He was looking forward to going with her to the target range. He knew that he would be sharing his meeting with her with his friends.

John shared what he figured was going down. He correctly made the point that Cutter was enjoying himself on money that had been advanced to him for this trip. He pointed out that the councilman was trying to avenge some long time grievance but really had no business making a challenge about who the executor of the trust should be.

He added that he thought that Samuel Ellington III was in it for the money and most likely had figured out how he could get control of "managing" the trust for Cutter.

They would both suggest that he, Cutter let them manage the trust and he could go back to Idaho and enjoy life. They would manage the trust for him and send money to him on a monthly basis.

Cutter was surprised that John had accurately described a conversation he had just that morning with Samuel and William.

He wondered how he had gotten that insight and asked as much.

Cutter turned to Alex as she commented that he would enjoy a few months of the cash flow but that very soon it would stop.

She commented that he had probably already signed the paperwork that put Samuel and William in the driver's seat. Now all that needed to happen was for the court to name Richard Cutter the executor and then they would have control and they would have the money.

She went on to tell him that in reality it did not matter because he would never get to be the executor.

First he had not had contact with the family for at least thirty years.

Second he had proved he could not manage his money by being behind on the credit cards he had, and he had at least three DUI's on record.

The judge would deny him the role of executorship.

The only reason he was enjoying the current moment was because Samuel Ellington III thought he was so smart and other people so dumb that he would get away with it.

He had no clue about the losing hand that he was holding.

Cutter said, "damn."

I swear you two were somehow listening to the meeting I was in this afternoon. He then shared that he had not signed anything yet but was scheduled to do so in the morning. He had been wanting to go to another lawyer to check out the arrangements they were pushing him to agree to.

John replied that he had just described what he knew of how the scam would work.

Cutter watched as Alex smiled and commented that she wanted to make him a deal.

She didn't want him to get screwed which if he went to court and won he would be.

She again said he didn't stand a chance in court.

The deal was she would take him and his gun to the firing range and the two of them could see who could hit the target.

If she won, he would pack his bags and go back to Idaho.

Cutter asked how she knew he had his gun.

He like her response of, "You're a lumber jack named Cutter from Idaho. A true lumber man always packs his gun."

John asked if he could be at the range too. He had no interest in shooting, but he wanted to watch.

Alex looked at her phone for the time. She put in a call and asked if she could have two positions before the range closed.

She would use her own weapon and ammo and so would the person with her.

She promised to pick up the casings and get rid of the targets.

Cutter was amazed that she had made arrangement so quickly, but he was eager to show his stuff. He hadn't shared the fact that he was a competitive shooter that almost always took first place.

He decided that it was time to boast a little and make her nervous.

Alex smiled and said that she was pleased to know that she had met a talented lumber man from Idaho.

Cutter smiled and followed her out of the bar.

Alex led the way to the police station. The range was to the back of the lot. It was clear when they entered the range that Alex was well known to everyone there.

They each set up their own targets.

He insisted that she go first.

Her smile caught him by surprise. She suggested that they shoot with their eyes closed.

He looked at her and said he had never done that before.

She replied that she would shoot with her eyes closed.

He could keep his eyes open.

He then was surprised that she told him that she would put one shot dead center and five shots around the edge of the bullseye.

He asked how he would know that she really had her eyes shut.

The range manager gave him the blind fold material to check out and suggest that he, Cutter, put it on Alex.

Cutter watched in amazement as Alex put her first shot dead center and then the five shots evenly spaced around the edge of the bullseye but in the center red side.

He knew he had met a master.

He took off her blind fold and checked to see that he could not see through it. He shook his head and said that it seemed impossible but now he knew why every person who attacked her was pushing up daisies.

Alex grinned at him and said it was his turn.

Three of his six shots hit dead center but three were at the white side of the center.

He listened as Alex said that what she had done with her eyes closed, John was going to do to Samuel Ellington III and the councilman.

She went on to say that John could put his legal shots dead center and he could do it with his eyes closed.

Cutter agreed that it would be a good time to get back to Idaho. He would enjoy his friends and put the pipe dream of quick money into the rearview mirror.

He said that he really disliked Ellington and hoped that he would get screwed. He really was such a jerk.

He asked if he could keep the target that Alex had used and if she would sign it.

Alex smiled and suggested that he keep his drinking to three shots at a time and use his skill with his gun on the shooting range to take as many additional shots as possible that he felt like taking.

She signed her target, shook his hand, and led the way out of the shooting range.

Cutter looked at her and said that he was going to take her advice and slow up on his drinking.

17 Playing Poker

John commented that he had never known anyone that could shoot like she did. He commented that it was no wonder Trey was willing to be her backup. He asked her how she had ever mastered shooting blind folded.

She said that she and her arm had an agreement. She would let it have its way as long as it knew where to shoot.

John laughed and said the he believed her.

She said that she did not know exactly how she had developed that capability. All that she knew was that she spent an hour a day at the range, so she knew that practice was a big part of it but she knew that she had some inherent natural talent that was a part of it.

John asked Alex to accompany him to meet with her old friend Samuel Ellington III. He had to retract the "old friend" comment when Alex asked if he really wanted her help or if he was trying to antagonize her.

He knew that Alex distained Samuel. He had been trying to inject humor into what his request. He as well distained Samuel and thought of him as a bad apple.

He commented to her that he would not want to play poker with her because he was sure he would lose to her but that he was going to play poker with Samuel and the case that Samuel was leading. He figured that like all bullies Samuel would fold when confronted with the obvious certainty of failure.

He listened as Alex agreed and asked when the poker game was to take place. He asked her to come over on Monday at one so that he could fill her in on her part and that they would go to Samuel's office that was a couple of blocks away and meet with him at two.

The information that Alex had Johnnie dug up was damming. If the councilman continued to be involved he might even face criminal charges.

Since Cutter had agreed to go back to Idaho, the case was dead. If Samuel insisted on going forward with the hearing, Cutter's roughhousing, and drinking background would be exposed and he would likely lose the challenge. It was also now clear that Cutter had never contacted Walter and Fiona Maninsky for more than thirty years. He was so distant that he should have no say about the money.

His claim after all the years to any of the money was ludicrous.

John organized his poker hand.

He would make a point of introducing Alex and remind Samuel of Alex's tremendous investigative powers.

He would then let him know that he knew the councilman was facilitating the connection with the long removed relative.

Finally, he would lay out the facts about this distant relative and remind Samuel of that it looked very much like a takeover scam that the councilman and he had cooked up to get control to several million dollars.

John planned to ensure that neither of them would have anything to do with managing the trust fund.

The weekend and Monday morning drove his patience to the edge. Hanna had helped by coming over to his house to make lunch and then go for a walk with him.

It was nice to be getting back to their romance.

On Monday, he skipped lunch and went for a walk to think through his approach. He had each fact typed up on his office letterhead. He had written up the document that would be used to prevent either the councilman or Samuel to have any involvement in the subsequent management of the trust fund.

The part he was mulling through was how to leverage Alex's participation. He remembered Samuel's involvement in the shooting incident where Mary Ellen Rambler was shot and killed. His presence at that particular event was notable in that Samuel had never been to one of her parties.

When she was shot Samuel rushed to try and save her and had ignored her husband Henry who was next to her. That seemed to indicate an affair that had taken place elsewhere.

He thought the best way was to introduce Alex and have Alex remind Samuel that the last time they had met was when she found him covered in Mary Ellen's blood.

Then he would share that she had provided the name of the councilman. He would give Samuel an official looking report that he would have Alex sign. He would then move on to identifying the distant relative and hand Samuel an official looking report that gave Cutter's history also signed by Alex.

He would close with the paperwork that blocked Samuel's involvement with the trust.

He was back in the office and had all the documents laid out. He hoped that Alex was willing to play along. He was doing nothing illegal. The documents would never get used because he could not submit them in court because they were not real.

Alex had indeed surfaced all the information in a manner that it could not be used in court, but he was making it appear that he could do so.

His support opened his door and ushered Alex in. His support was smiling and said that she had gotten Cincinnati's Black Annie Oakley's autograph for herself and for her nieces.

John commented that he would try to get an autograph for his nephews.

He looked at Alex and commented that he had not been aware of her national reputation.

She replied that she hadn't known either.

He thanked her for being willing to be his poker playing partner. He then shared his plan and showed Alex each of his documents.

Alex suggested that they have a notary authenticate the signature to make it look more official.

He immediately called in his support and asked her to get Hanna to come and witness Alex's signature. Again, everything was legal. The witnesses were only witnessing the signature and not involved with the content of the document.

The walk to Samuel's office only took a few minutes. They approached the receptionist that wore a name plate with Linda on it.

He was surprised to receive a broad smile. She pointed to Alex and said she knew who she was and that she should simply shoot Samuel between the eyes and get it over with.

He enjoyed Alex's reply of "I see you love him too" and Linda's reply that it had nothing to do with love but that she worked for him because he paid her twice as much as she could make anywhere else.

She knocked on the office door and then opened and led them in.

John watched as Samuel looked into the mirror as he stood up and straightened out his jacked before stepping around the desk to greet them. He thought immediately that the poker game would be fun and that he had the winning hand.

He knew how to pace and reveal it in a nice slow manner that would drive Samuel crazy.

John watched as Samuel recognized Alex. It seemed that some color left his face. He wondered what was going through Samuel's mind. He was sure that Samuel recognized a true opponent as he looked at Alex.

John hoped he would be so distracted that he would not realize he was being taken.

John sat down as Alex commented on the fact that Samuel had continued his practice in Cincinnati. She guessed that he was still enjoying the rich ladies he had met at the Rambler's party.

Samuel replied that he had reformed his way and was on the straight and narrow with a permanent companion.

John then started the poker game. He watched Samuel and decided that he had a sharp opponent. However, he caught the signs of confidence going slowly away. The tell was the notary public imprint that Samuel fingered as each document was passed to him.

Alex was relatively quiet, but she would periodically make a comment like, "I wonder what a Cincinnati Council member would think about being investigated for participating in a scam." She also commented on how a heavy drinking lumberman would fare when in the witness seat during the trial.

The comments were timed exactly when Samuel was fingering the notary imprint.

John realized that Alex was in tune with Samuel's reaction to the documents.

John gathered all the documents he had brought and thanked Samuel for his time. He finished by saying that if the case was dropped everything that had been discussed would not become public knowledge. However, if it went forward everything would move into the public domain.

He suggested that Samuel could close down the case by canceling the court date and issuing a statement that the challenge was being withdrawn.

John did not wait for a reply but stood up and led the way to the door. Once outside he looked at Alex and thanked her for her participation.

He said he wished he could listen to who Samuel was talking to.

He almost fell over when Alex smiled and said that he would know as soon as her analyst or partner called her.

Later he learned that the call had gone to the council man and the two had agreed to drop the case.

18 Grand Jury

*A*lex listened to the prosecutor as he explained that each of the former Altar boys had been great witnesses that had made a very positive impression. He said that each of them had stood in front of the jury and had presented their information as if they were seasoned speakers.

He was surprised how effective they had been.

He felt that the twenty-three members of the Grand Jury would hold few doubts about recommending a trial. It was always hard to read their reaction but he again said that the two witnesses had both scored three pointers. It was a topic that made everyone put on a straight face and show little emotion.

She was to be the next person to share her experience with the Grand Jury. They already had the documents that Eduardo, Bill, Travis, and Trey had all written and signed.

The video Trey had taken with his I-phone would be shown to them for the first time when she was in the room. She would provide the supporting dialogue and answer the questions the jury might pose.

She was getting her last-minute coaching. It was clear to her that Hanna and the prosecutor were nervous about the presentation. Hanna commented that she wished she could be in the room but made the point that it was not allowed.

Alex felt at ease.

She was sure that the video that had surprised her when she had first seen it would convince the jury that a crime that deserved to be prosecuted had been committed. It might not be pedophile behavior, but it would be strong enough to put Father Chris behind bars for a long time.

The prosecutor had explained that video would be shown on the largest screen he had been able to obtain. He had rented it from a warehouse where they tracked delivery semitrucks across the entire US.

It was huge!

He had watched the video at that scale and had been blown away by the impact that it had on him.

He wanted to make sure Alex was prepared.

He went on to explain that he would show it when she was in the chamber and then use it again when Father Chris was before the Grand Jury on the following day.

He asked if Father Chris had ever seen the video.

Alex said that she had not shown him the video.

Alex reassured Hanna that she was relaxed about standing in front of the twenty-three jurists.

As they were waiting she got a call from the Chief who had the whole team in his office on speaker phone. They all told her to knock them dead.

Hanna commented that Alex had a blockbuster team.

The prosecutor went in to greet the jury and to explain that the next presentation was not about Father Chris's action in the long past but about his actions in the past few weeks.

Father Chris had tried to kill an officer of the law.

He watched the reaction that statement had on the jury. It was clear that they had not expected that twist in the case.

Alex stood and followed the person that led her to a stand where she faced the Grand Jury.

She introduced herself and stated that everything that she would share with them was documented and had followed the strict rule of evidence handling and traceability.

She looked at the size of the screen and was glad that the prosecutor had described its size. To say it was huge was insufficient.

It was humongous!

The prosecutor nodded and the scene in the Church began to play.

Alex explained her slow walk up the center aisle and why she looked to the left and then to the right down along the space between the pews. She did not want to be surprised by a side attack.

She was looking left when Father Chris came swiftly across the Altar level. The weapon he was carrying was immediately obvious and the huge screen seemed to make it seem ever more ominous than she remembered it.

She seemed to immediately drop between the pews to her right as the axe head missed her by mere inches.

She stopped for a few seconds as the members in the jury stand all let out a gasp. She shared the fact that when she had seen how close the Father had come she said a prayer of thanks because she thought of it as a miracle.

She continued and commented that she had been surprised by her next move where she in essence used a pole-vaulting flip over the front pew and as she was going over her left hand drew her belt knife and as she came down, she plunged it into Father Chris's leg.

Her voice could clearly be heard shouting, "Don't shoot, Don't shoot." She next stood up and hit Father Chris with the edge of her hand across the side of his neck. She explained that it happened so fast that she had reacted strictly by reflex. She said that afterwards she had immediately checked the Father's vital signs to make sure he was still breathing.

As the video panned across the Altar level it highlighted her checking Father Chris for vitals and then focused on the ax head stuck on the side of the front pew.

She pointed out that Father Chris had been trying to free the ax so he could use it again.

She expect questions but several of the jurors said they wanted to see it again before questioning her. They had the video stopped as Alex pulled the knife from the buckle of her belt.

One of the Jurors asked the size of the blade and gave a whistle when Alex pulled out the blade that was all of two inches long and had a handle that had to be held between two fingers. He commented that it did not seem to be very dangerous and certainly not an attack weapon.

She fielded the question that with her reputation as being a great marksman with her service revolver why she had not shot Father Chris.

She replied that if she had then the Grand Jury would not have been needed.

Alex replied that she had not been thinking that far ahead. She, her partner, and Eduardo their escort while in Mexico, had all agreed that it would have been inappropriate to us a gun while in church. That is why she shouted for them not to shoot as she was in the process of getting Father Chris out of action.

She explained that there was a large park in front of the Cathedral that she kept referring to as a church. There were many people enjoying the late afternoon. Somehow the word got out that Father Jones, as he was known to them, was a pedophile. They were shouting loudly for him to come out.

Alex said that Eduardo had volunteered to delay the mob as long as he could.

Alex explained that she and Trey her partner, with some help, were able to get the ax back to its stand and to wipe up the blood from the floor. She was the last one out and was just able to get out of sight as the mob burst through the door.

Father Chris required a tourniquet on his leg. The drive back to her friends compound took almost four hours. When they arrived, there was a person that skillfully sealed the artery that had been nicked and that would have been the end of the situation but somehow the word got out locally that Father Jones was in the compound.

She, her partner, and Father Chris who was transported on a flatbed wheelbarrow left the compound and made their way down through the forest to a point where Eduardo had the car waiting for them.

She then described the four-hour journey to El Paso where Father Chris had the choice to stay in Mexico where he would have been arrested by Eduardo and sent to a Mexican prison to await trial or to willingly be escorted into the US by her.

Father Chris had chosen to come into the US with her. His consent was documented at the Mexican side of the border before he crossed into the US with her.

She fielded a few more questions from the jury and then the prosecutor thanked her, and she was escorted from the chamber.

She and Hanna were sitting in the building cafeteria when he approached and commented that Alex had sealed Father Chris's fate.

He commented that he had already met with Father Chris and his lawyer the previous day and had been surprised that Father Chris was still willing to go in front of the Grand Jury. Father Chris planned to make his case that he had been pressured to come back to the US and that he should not need to be in front of the Jury.

It was a few days later that the prosecutor called and let Alex know that ninety per cent of the Grand Jury had recommended that Father Chris stand trial for his indiscretions and for the attack on an officer of the law.

He shared that he had been able to get a judge to take the case in two weeks.

Alex meanwhile heard from John that Samuel Ellington had withdrawn his case.

John shared with her that Father Chris's attorney communicated to Hanna that his client wanted to plead guilty and would do so if he would be sent to a low security white collar prison. He was willing to accept a twenty-year sentence. Such a sentence would most likely mean he would die in prison.

John asked if such a deal would be alright with Alex. He was certain that he could win an even longer sentence for his attack on her.

Alex replied that perhaps Father Chris would be able to find some solace in helping others while he served his time. She asked John how he felt about such a deal. She was glad to hear John say that he had forgiven Father Chris a long time ago.

The successful end of the two cases meant that Alex had once again set a record in both the short time to solve a complex case and then to be able to take advantage of getting to celebrate with her team.

19 Closure Celebration

*J*ohn felt a weight lift off his shoulders. He had thought that he had left the days as an Altar boy behind, but he now knew that he had continued to carry the hurt deep inside.

His discussion with Hanna about a thirty-year sentence and placement in a low security prison had surfaced some of the hurt. He figured that it was good for it to come out.

He was sure that Alex had provided the evidence that had sealed Father Chris's fate. She had also guided and helped close the trust manager case that he had been working on. He owed her more than money could pay.

He had learned that she had millions in a trust that provided aid to an organization she had established called "Open Hands."

The organization focused on helping abused women in need. He now saw her as that rare person that seemed self-balanced, extremely talented, humble, and focused on helping others.

He felt she would make an excellent psychiatrist because she listened so well that, as he had learned, a person just naturally responds to her presence and attitude.

John thought about her comment that she was in the field that allowed her to bring in the bad guys so that people like himself could do their job and get justice for the rest of society. She was truly a talent that he would try to tap into in the future. He now knew how to get a request to her boss in a manner that would not upset him.

He had taken the next step with Hanna. He had proposed to her and taken her to see the home in Indian Hill that he planned to buy.

Hanna had said yes and that she loved the house. She commented that it was a bit too large, but it was beautiful.

They had set a date and had set a celebration party to let their friends know about the proposal.

The invitation list grew to include more than one hundred people.

Hanna insisted that Alex and all of the people that were on her team be invited.

Alex and Matt were having breakfast when Johnnie knocked on the door. He came in and shared that he had just opened up an invitation from John to a celebration party.

He asked if Alex was planning on accepting her invitation.

Alex got up and went over to a pile of mail. She had the habit of waiting until the weekend to process her mail. She knew that most of what she got was junk mail.

She sorted through the pile and found the invitation from John.

John had put a personal touch to the invitation and said that the party had two purposes. One was to thank her for delivering solutions on both of the cases and the second was to announce his engagement to Hanna.

Alex shared her invitation with Matt and asked him if he wanted to make it a two engagement announcement.

She looked at Matt as it dawned on him that she had just proposed to him.

The smile that came to his face was like a beacon of happiness. He reached into his pocket and pulled out a ring case. He said he had carried it on every date that he had been on with her. He had been hesitant to make the proposal because he feared being rejected.

Alex pulled him to her and gave him a kiss.

Johnnie let out a loud hurrah and said he could not believe that he had been present for such a great occasion. He said he had to leave to let Mary know about both the invitation and the proposal.

He said he planned to call everyone they knew.

Alex smiled as Matt got down on one knee and put the engagement ring on her finger.

She heard Johnnie let out another hurrah and say that he had captured the moment on his phone. He was sending it out as evidence. He said he would protect the chain and make sure it was admissible in court.

Alex looked at her ring finger and gave Matt another kiss.

She said that it would be great to go home to her parents and go fishing. She asked if he was interested in going.

Matt smiled and asked if she was working any cases at the moment.

When Alex said no, he smiled and said that then he would love to go fishing.

Little did Alex know that her next case would take place very close to where she lived and would make her an official Illinois State Marshall and would put her on deaths door only to be saved by the Angel on the Hill.

The End

Preview: Windy City

1: Inside Man

The sun was threatening to come over the horizon. The misty fog hanging over the scene of the shooting that gave it the feeling of evil. This feeling of evil, lurking in wait, was not unique to only the Windy City but universal in both large and small cities. The history of this evil was rooted in the history of mankind. It was the evil of projecting hate for those that were different.

Power was always a key differentiator. With power came wealth and often wealth ushered in power. Those in power looked down upon those below them. The discrimination that resulted was usually limited to making those below suffer by making them give more money to the rich.

The current evil that was in action was that of white against brown of any shade. It had been perpetrated by two men in blue for no other reason than they felt it was their right.

Jesse Franklin, deputy chief of police, ducked under the yellow security tape as he held out his badge for the young policewoman.

He had recently hired her and assigned her to this duty. He was sure this was her first murder crime scene.

The yellow taped area blocked off most of the corner of the intersection in a way that allowed traffic to be guided around the scene. An older model black Ford was at the center of the scene.

He walked over to the car and took in the young black man sitting in a pool of blood looking as if he were sleeping. He saw that a gun was still in the driver's right hand.

For a moment he watched the coroner examine the body of the driver. He noted that the blood pooled in the driver's seat had run down the drivers left leg. Jesse was sure that the driver had bled to death.

The driver was dressed as if he were going out for a run. He was not dressed as the typical drug dealer that Jesse normally saw.

The dispatcher had received a call about a drug dealer that had resisted arrest.

Jesse did not see a drug dealer.

He asked the coroner about the shooting.

The coroner told him that the man had been shot three times, once in the head and twice in the chest. He used his hand to show that the shots were from the driver's left side at what looked like a downward angle.

He went on and said that the wounds seemed to indicate the man had been shot while sitting in the driver's seat.

He leaned the driver up against the wheel and used a pointer and pushed it into what appeared to be a bullet hole.

The coroner said that they would likely find a bullet somewhere in the seat back.

What was clear to Jesse was that a young dead black man was about to be zipped into a body bag that the coroner's assistant had just wheeled up to the car.

He had seen too many similar cases. Usually, they were easier to accept as drug deals gone wrong. This scene and the coroner's showing him what appeared to be a bullet hole in the seat back pointed him to two rogue cops.

He looked around and saw the two policemen that had been involved. They were part of the group of cops that did a variety of shady errands that Jesse arranged for the Chicago Mafia. He wondered about this situation and what had really gone down.

He walked over and asked what had happened.

The story from the two police officers was that they had approached the car because of a broken taillight. They claimed the driver had opened the door of the vehicle and raised his gun to shoot at them. They shouted for him to drop his gun and when he didn't, they shot him, and he fell back into the driver's seat.

They went on to say that they had found a stash of drugs on the passenger side floor.

Jesse saw through the lie. He was sure the two had set up the scene to make it look like they had shot a drug dealer. He decided not to challenge the two but to wait for the coroner's report before taking any action.

He knew that at a minimum he would assign these two to some district where they would not be involved in any more killing of young black men. The two would get the standard two weeks desk duty and then he would return them to street duty. At the moment that was all that he planned to do with the case.

He was glad that it was Friday, and he would not have to deal with the details of the incident until Monday.

He looked around the scene before leaving. The sun had broken over the horizon and had made the fluffy white clouds appear. He loved the day night cycle and the atmosphere of living by the lake.

When he arrived back to his office, the flashing light on his phone seemed to emulate the flashing light of a police car. He really disliked that light. He pressed the button to hear the message. He let out an internal groan when he recognized it as a coded message from the office of the Chicago Mafia Boss, Gennaro Visentino.

Jesse thought of Gennaro as a true mafia god father figure.

He really did not need any complications on an already screwed up Friday morning. He knew that he would have to contact him to see what Gennaro had in mind.

He turned off the voice mail. He opened his desk drawer and extracted one of his many burner phones from the back. He then let his support know that he was going for a quick walk to unwind.

He was following a standard routine that he had practiced for many years. He never made calls to Gennaro from his office, and he never used the same phone more than once.

He walked toward the Lake and made his call.

Gennaro graciously thanked him for a quick response. It always impressed Jesse that Gennaro was always polite. Jesse also knew that Gennaro was just as deadly as he was polite.

What Gennaro had to say had his hair standing on end. It seemed that the office of the Illinois Lieutenant Governor was seeking to hire a Cincinnati police detective, Alex Evercrest, to investigate corruption in the Chicago police department.

This detective had earned national recognition for her ability to resolve every case she had been assigned to. She had experienced multiple attempts on her life and was recognized as a dead shot when she pulled her weapon.

Alarm bells went off in Jesse's head.

Jesse knew about one of her cases, just a couple of years ago, that had involved a coal barge that had lit up the Chicago skyline. Single handedly she had taken out an attack helicopter and destroyed a tug and coal barge.

The report was that she had been unarmed and fishing when the attack began, and she had been unarmed when the DEA greeted her on her return to the fishing dock. She claimed that she had been fishing and knew nothing about the burning barge.

The body count was said to be at least six, but no bodies had ever been recovered.

He brought his attention into focus as the mafia boss asked him to call her and warn her not to accept the assignment. Gennaro wanted Jesse to make it clear in no uncertain terms that accepting the offer would mean certain retribution by the Chicago Mafia. She was to understand that there would be not second chance to change her mind.

Jesse reacted negatively to making a call threatening the detectives life.

He did not want to be the one to make the call, but this was not a situation that he could say no to.

He preferred a controlled beating that allowed the person to feel the pain personally and decide to obey Gennaro.

He had alarm bells going off in his head.

He would proceed with ultimate caution.

He had no other choice. He agreed to make the call.

The weekend was not going to be as relaxing as he had planned. He had a nagging feeling about the situation. He had called an acquaintance on the Cincinnati police force and asked about the Black detective.

He learned that she always got the people involved in the case she was assigned to solve. He learned that she was very likeable and friendly and that her opponents seemed to underestimate her.

That evening he took a sleeping pill and went to sleep. Even then he woke up several times.

The rest of the weekend seemed to drag. He went online and reviewed the stories about the black detective that he found in the national news snippets. It gave him indigestion. He took the pills for indigestion and heart burn, but they did him no good.

After reviewing her past accomplishments, he knew that she would not scare. He was certain that his call would be a waste of time.

He kept going over what he would say in warning. He intuitively knew that it did not matter what or how he would say it and that she had a track record that said she did not scare.

Why make the call? He remembered throwing a rock at a huge hornet's paper nest and watching the immediate surge of a black stream of small hornets heading straight for him. They somehow were able to follow the trajectory of the rock.

He had the feeling that the phone call would be like throwing a stone at just as dangerous black detective.

He expected that this detective would follow the money trail. He felt that his lifestyle would put him under the magnifying glass. He was living in a luxury condominium and had a forty-five-foot yacht anchored in Burnham harbor.

He had let his boss know about his "family inheritance" so that he could move into the luxury condo. He later had purchased the yacht. He had let his associates at the station know that his parents had left him a small fortune. He had been told that he was a lucky person to have parents that had been frugal and set him up for the good life.

There had been no inheritance, but it provided the cover he needed. The truth was he had to use his own money to pay for his parents funerals.

He had told his wife the same story about an inheritance. She had been surprised because she did not think his parents had much money to leave him, but she did not question it.

She loved the three thousand square foot condo he had leased and partying on the yacht.

She did not care much about going out of the harbor to go fishing so he usually did that with some of his work associates. He had few personal friends and he kept it that way so that he did not have to explain his lifestyle.

All of his property, including a luxury condo in Miami, was registered under his wife's maiden name.

He felt confident in having covered his trail. He had made much of it public and the real money was offshore.

He had made sure that his personal bank account balanced with the income he made. He and his wife had modest investments in an IRA.

The money he "earned" with the mafia connection went to an offshore account in the Caymans and he seldom tapped into it. He was waiting until he left the department before touching it.

Jesse felt that he was secure in his personal position but what he had learned about Alex Evercrest's ability worried him. He hoped that he would not have to throw too many of the cops that did his bidding under the bus. It would be bad for his cash flow.

He came in on Monday and around nine he took one of his burner phones and went out for a walk.

He called the Cincinnati police station and asked for Alex Evercrest. He was on hold for a short time and then he heard a pleasant voice say, "May all be well with you, this is Alex how may I help you?" He knew that in any other situation he would like her. She had perfect diction and it was clear she was very friendly.

The hornets coming out of their nest flashed in his mind.

He tried to hide his real voice by deepening his tone, he told her that accepting a position to root out corruption in the Chicago police force would endanger her life and the lives of her loved ones.

He was surprised at her chuckle and her response of thanking him for helping her make up her mind. She then went on to say that the two of them would soon meet and he should be ready to spend a great portion of his future life behind bars. He then heard a click.

She had ended the call!

Her response put him in as state of panic. She had reacted in a much more aggressive way than he had expected. And she seemed so sure she would know who he was.

He took out a second burner phone and called Gennaro and let him know that his call had landed on deaf ears and that the Cincinnati detective had indicated she planned to accept coming to Chicago to root out the spoiled eggs that were on the police force.

He looked out toward the lake as the silence reverberated through his head.

He felt some sense of relief when he heard Gennaro say that he would take care of the Cincinnati detective and that he should relax because she would never make it to Chicago.

He liked the way Gennaro was choosing to deal with the situation. He envisioned a fly being splattered by a fly swatter.

He returned to the office. His support handed him the coroner's initial report. He carefully read through it and knew that the two cops had killed an innocent man. He put in a call to check on the victim's previous arrest records. There were none. He knew of no drug dealers with no arrest records.

A call from the Internal Affairs letting him know that they were looking into the shooting made it clear that he needed to get the two officers off the force. He knew Internal Affairs would find out the same information that he had.

He called in the two cops. He asked them again to tell him what had happened. It was clear that the two had spent the morning embellishing their story.

They handed him a written report. They had the black driver getting out of the car and then reaching for his gun. They had immediately called out, "police, you are under arrest and then as his gun came out, one of them had shot him twice in the chest and the other shot him once in the head.

As he listened, he picked up the coroner's report that clearly indicated the shots had been at an angle that indicated the shooters were standing and shooting down at the victim.

The two officers had made up their stories. They were lying to him. It seemed to him that the two probably killed an innocent person and made it look like a drug bust.

He looked at them and told them to read the coroner's report and that they had an appointment with Internal Affairs. He advised them to improve their story telling and that at least the lies should match the facts that were in the Coroner's report.

He then suggested they resign, walk out of the office, and go find jobs elsewhere.

He asked them for their guns and assigned them to two weeks of desk duty. He was washing his hands of their case. He was throwing them under the bus.

The two said that they were resigning and would find jobs elsewhere.

He was relieved. He felt he had more important things to worry about.

He had no idea that the more important worry was coming at him faster than he anticipated. He was totally blind to the fact that Alex Evercrest's mother was the one that had created the tsunami of catastrophes that was about to overtake his life.

He should have paid closer attention to the name of the lawyer that had asked for the police reports on the case cops who were being prosecuted for shooting a black driver of a car stopped for speeding. If he had paid closer attention, he would have linked Alex Evercrest with her mother, Rose Ann Evercrest, the lawyer who had repeatedly asked for information that he had blocked.

2 Connections

ose Anne took pride in winning her cases for her clients. Her practice grew as her win record became known. She represented many affluent white clients but made it a policy that she would represent an equal number of black or people of color. Her practice of doing ten percent pro-bono work turned out to be the best public advertisement that she had for her business. She made a point that her pro-bon work also crossed the color barrier and made sure that at least seventy percent went for those most discriminated against.

She had several young lawyers that she had hired because she felt they were among the best she could find. She had always made the claim that the best people represented the least expense for a business because their successes generated more income. Her monetary compensation for the best put her employees among the highest paid in the Chicago legal system. It also made them among the most loyal employees.

Rose-Anne knew many of the details of Alex's successful cases. She had been horrified by the flaming spectacle that Alex had lived through out on the lake. She had been aboard the yacht that carried the entire Cincinnati detective unit out to go fishing. Then as they were fishing, and she watched in amazement as Alex dodged bullets to get everyone to safety and then Alex had used her skill to disable the speed boat of the attacker. When they got to the peer, she saw the blood dripping from Alex's gun hand as Alex ran up the dock to try to stop the attacker. She then realized that her daughter was phenomenal, and she was an attack dog when threatened.

She was aware of and thought that Alex had even taken out the leader of the Gulf Cartel. That was a case where Trey had almost been killed and Alex was out for payback. She however knew that after that case, a new cartel boss made his appearance.

Rose Anne had come to realize that her daughter was both brilliant in mind and deadly in fighting crime and she was one of the best across the entire country.

When she learned that a local Cincinnati lawyer had been able to get her to help him on two cases, Rose Ann decided that she would see if she could arrange for Alex to deal with the broken Chicago Police force.

She was frustrated with dealing with the case of three policemen accused of killing an innocent driver that had been stopped for speeding.

The shooting had been captured on video from an overpass by a person who happened to be walking across at the time of the arrest. The video seemed to indicate that it would be an open and shut case.

After taking on the case, she had asked for the police reports and for any other evidence that had been gathered. She was stonewalled. She came up empty handed.

She had submitted her request to the top Chicago Police leaders with no result.

She decided that something had to be done to clean up the system. The police department seemed to have become a law onto itself. They did whatever they wanted.

She reached out to her college roommate friend, Jane Stradford, who had been elected as the Illinois Lieutenant Governor.

The two agreed that a lucrative offer for Alex's services to come for a special assignment to root out corrupt police was a great idea.

Jane commented that it would stretch her budget but if she could make a dent in eliminating the corruption, she felt it would be worth it. She said that she would make the best offer that she could and hoped that it would be attractive to both Alex and her bosses.

Jane commented that she knew how tight her budget was and figured that the police budget in Cincinnati would be just as tight and they would welcome a generous financial arrangement.

She put together the offer and sent it out so it would be in Alex's boss's hands on Monday morning.

On Monday both of them were surprised that Alex's initial inclination was to turn down the offer but that she would spend the day to think about it and consider it.

Rose-Anne let Russel know about her request to have Alex come to Chicago to root out bad cops and about Alex's hesitation.

He had responded that he thought as a mother she should not be asking her daughter to take on the Chicago mafia.

It was as dangerous as facing a helicopter gunship with a fishing pole.

Rose Anne's response was that she had not asked her to take on the Mafia but to look for bad cops.

Russel replied with a question, "Who do you think bad cops work for? Their Mafia bosses will not take it lightly and they control their environment with violence."

This stopped the reply she had been thinking of giving him because of his gunship remark. She had overlooked that obvious Mafia connection.

She was disturbed as she walked away after the discussion.

Not long after, her Alex chimes came from her phone.

When Alex asked if she had been the catalyst that had triggered the request for her services from the Illinois Lieutenant Governor's office, she replied that she indeed had been but that she was now thinking it was not such a good idea.

She told Alex to turn down the request.

She was not expecting to hear Alex laugh and reply that she intended to accept on the condition that she and her detective partner were hired by the Lieutenant Governor and would be employees of the state of Illinois for as long as the assignment lasted. She was encouraging her boss to accept the lucrative compensation offer for such an arrangement.

Rose-Anne again said that she was sorry about having the request made and tried to dissuade Alex, but she knew that she had no chance of do so.

She again heard Alex laugh and was told that the price of having thought of such an arrangement was that she planned to work from home.

Rose Anne felt great about that the idea but kept quiet.

She listened as Alex went on and let her know that Trey's family would be coming up on weekends to stay at the house. They would be using one to the bedrooms.

Alex also mentioned that her dad should consider going fishing on most weekends.

Rose Anne liked everything she heard.

She was now a concerned mother versus the successful prosecutor that had recruited her daughter into a dangerous role. She said that she would do all she could to make sure Alex would get the support she needed.

Rose-Anne called Jane and shared the fact that Alex would only accept the request if she and her current partner were hired by the Lieutenant Governor's office for a one-year period of pay at their current salary and that the original monetary offer was to be separately given to the Cincinnati Detective office.

Rose-Ann listened as Jane replied that for her it was a no brainer. She would love to have someone like Alex working for her department for a year. However, she would need to check her budget to see how she would work it out.

Work sucked Rose-Anne back in and she was consumed in trying to get the information she needed to proceed with the case against the three policemen.

She requested a delay of the trial until the documents she needed were made available. The judge agreed to a two-month delay. It was the breather she was looking for.

She let her staff know about the delay and asked them to handle the smaller cases that were underway.

She planned to use the week to prepare for Alex and Trey's arrival.

She turned her attention to getting the house ready.

Rose-Anne was warming to the idea of having Alex working from home and wondered how long such an arrangement would last. She hoped that it would indeed be a year.

She watched as Russel tuned and polished Alex's twelve-cylinder Jaguar. They both knew that it was a treasure that Alex loved.

She then noted that he also inspected and prepared all the fishing equipment. Fishing had been an activity that he and Alex had shared and enjoyed since she was a little girl.

She listened as he called to have their boat tuned up and put back in the water. The owner of the boat docks at the harbor was almost as excited as Russel about having Alex back to go fishing and even offered his personal yacht and jokingly commented that he only asked that this time it be returned without bullet holes in it. This was his reference to the last time he had rented the boat to Russel when the entire Cincinnati detective team had gone fishing and a shooter had put at least a dozen holes into the boat.

Rose Ann continued to worry but she knew that Alex would call her own shots and make her own deal.

She had no idea of the risk and the carnage that Alex was about to experience. And she had no idea about the kind of loyal and powerful supporters Alex was surrounded by.

She would have been pleased to know that Alex's boss Bruce, Chief of Detectives, and his wife Mary-Ann thought of Alex as the daughter they never had and they were constantly discussing how to keep her safe.

Thank You for reading this far.

To continue Reading Windy City go to:

https://www.remwriter95.net/

About the Author

Ronald E. Mueller
remwriter95@gmail.com

Ron grew up in what is now Flint River State Park in Southeast Iowa. The 170-year-old house Ron lived in is built into a hillside. It faces a 125-foot-high cliff towering over the little Flint River. The house and the land talked to him about; the passing of time, the struggle to conquer the land, the struggles people faced and the wonder of nature.

He climbed the cliffs, crawled into the caves, dove from the swimming rock, collected clams from the bottom of the pond, gigged and skinned frogs for their legs. He trapped muskrats for fur, hunted raccoon in the dead of night, and with only a stick hunted rabbits in the dead of winter.

His young life was outdoors, and nature tested him.

He walked to a one room stone schoolhouse uphill both ways. A stern but warm-hearted teacher, Mrs. Henry was instrumental in shaping his character as she shepherded him from the fourth to the eighth grade.

It was a great way to grow up.

Ron graduated from Burlington, High School, went to Vietnam in the Navy. He graduated from The University of South Florida with an master's degree in engineering, worked for thirty eight years for Procter and Gamble, traveled around the world thirty times.

He has remained happily married for more than fifty years. His daughter and his two sons are all successful and his three grandchildren have all graduated.

His wife has humored and supported him as he became a full time professional story teller.

He has come to realize that he is, what is known as, a Cozy writer. Excitement and adventure but little guts and gore. His heroine or hero suffer a little but live happily ever after.

His experiences inter-twined with snippets of fantasy lend themselves to the adventures he leads the reader through.

Books by the Author

Fiction Series
The Alex Evercrest Series
The River Front
The Girl on The Grill
Missing
Maggot
Racist
Votive Candles
Windy City
Country Road
Pool of Blood
Sins of the Daughter
Body Parts
The Skull Collector
The Vanishing
The Shadow Fighter
Moonshine
Grief's Trajectory
The Magic Touch
Northern Lights
Alex Evercrest Heroine
Alex Evercrest Collection Two
New Direction
A Family Affair
Disruption
The St. Lebuinnus Church Murder

A Brian O'Neil Novel
Hawaiian Phoenix
Moon Curser
Death Broker

The Problem Solver Series
Solutions
Drug Lords
Border Crosser
The Problem Solver Collection

The Taelo Series
Taelo: The Early Years
Taelo: The Golden Feather
Taelo: Journey of Discovery
Taelo: Dangerous Passage
Taelo: Condor Clan Slingers
Taelo: Circumvention
Taelo: The Journey of Sages
Taelo: Collection
Taelo: Future Leaders Journey

A Taelo Story:
White Swan and Quiet Pheasant
The Child's Name
Floating Cloud
Quiet Rabbit
Busy Bee
Little Otter & Talking Wren
Broken Spear
Burley Bear & Meadow Flower
Taelo Story Collection

Science Fiction
The Savitar Series:
Journey's End
Savitar
Confluence
Savitar Series Collection

Bram Nielson Series
The Fold
The Message
Fold Wormhole
Negative Fold
Ripples in Time
Bram Nielson Collection

Single Science Fiction Books:
Current Past and Future
The Event
The Door
Viajante 7

Published by: Around the World Publishing LLC.

https://www.Remwriter95.net/